"And what do you owe me?" Adam whispered.

"Not a thing," Bridgette tried to snap, but her voice trembled.

Slowly Adam's lips descended, touching hers gently but sending a reaction of megaton strength rocketing through her body. His kiss claimed her, pushing her over the brink into the hot, blinding land Adam's kisses had always taken her to. She wanted him. After all these months, she wanted him desperately. His fingers had slipped under her clothes and were exploring the swell of her breasts. Ever so slowly his hands swept along her silky skin, reminding her how much she still belonged to him.

Suddenly she was aroused from the unreal world she'd entered. With all her strength Bridgette pushed him back. "Satisfied?" she asked bitterly.

"Oh, I wouldn't say that just yet," he replied softly, meaningfully.

Bridgette's eyes narrowed. "That's all you'll get, Mr. Reeves. I haven't sat here for eleven months just waiting for you to come back to me."

Dear Reader:

As the months go by, we continue to receive word from you that SECOND CHANCE AT LOVE romances are providing you with the kind of romantic entertainment you're looking for. In your letters you've voiced enthusiastic support for SECOND CHANCE AT LOVE, you've shared your thoughts on how personally meaningful the books are, and you've suggested ideas and changes for future books. Although we can't always reply to your letters as quickly as we'd like, please be assured that we appreciate your comments. Your thoughts are all-important to us!

We're glad many of you have come to associate SECOND CHANCE AT LOVE books with our butterfly trademark. We think the butterfly is a perfect symbol of the reaffirmation of life and thrilling new love that SECOND CHANCE AT LOVE heroines and heroes find together in each story. We hope you keep asking for the ''butterfly books,'' and that, when you buy one—whether by a favorite author or a talented new writer—you're sure of a good read. You can trust all SECOND CHANCE AT LOVE books to live up to the high standards of romantic fiction you've come to expect.

So happy reading, and keep your letters coming!

With warm wishes,

Ellen Edwards

Ellen Edwards
SECOND CHANCE AT LOVE
The Berkley/Jove Publishing Group
200 Madison Avenue
New York, NY 10016

SCENES
FROM THE HEART
MARIE CHARLES

**SECOND CHANCE AT LOVE
BOOK**

SCENES FROM THE HEART

First edition published March 1983

First printing

"Second Chance at Love" and the butterfly emblem are trademarks belonging to Jove Publications, Inc.

Printed in the United States of America

Second Chance at Love books are published by
The Berkley/Jove Publishing Group
200 Madison Avenue, New York, NY 10016

To Ellen Edwards,
with thanks
for making it
better.

SCENES
FROM THE HEART

1

BRIDGETTE SANTANIELLO SAT in the sun-drenched living room of her spacious Beverly Hills house and stared ahead with unseeing eyes. Fear, anger, hurt, and lingering feelings of love all raged within her. She tried to ignore them so that she could focus her attention on the man who had been her literary agent since the beginning of her career as a screenwriter.

"Do I have to, Harry?" she asked unhappily.

The short, round man licked his upper lip. "You are the only one of my clients who has never made me pull out my hair," he said, running his hand along his bald pate, which was surrounded by just a hint of reddish hair.

"I wouldn't be asking you to do this if there were any other way. I know how you feel about working with Adam," he added sympathetically.

Did he? Did he really know what he was asking her to do? Bridgette wondered. Seeing Adam again would rip open wounds that hadn't even healed yet. She bit her lip.

"The studio just announced that he's been made the new film director. He's the best one for the job, and you need a hit just as much as the studio does," Harry reminded her. "Your last picture just broke even. That doesn't sit well with the board of directors."

"But it wasn't my fault that the director went over budget and brought it in three weeks behind schedule," she protested.

Harry shrugged. "The director said it was because of your 'fancy scenes.' And the studio believed him."

Bridgette winced. Since the so-called failure of the last movie based on her screenplay, her insecurities had grown unmanageable, engulfing her like private devils. It had been a terrible year. First, there had been the divorce, then all those problems with her screenplay, and now this.

Bridgette dug deep for the bravado that had sustained her through difficult times in the past, but it eluded her. "I don't think I can face Adam," she said, looking down at her tightly clasped hands. The very thought of working with her ex-husband made them tremble, which made her angry with herself. What was she, a frightened jellyfish?

"Bridgette," Harry said softly, struggling out of his chair, "it's not as if I'm asking you to live with the man." He placed a hand on her shoulder.

"I'll probably have to go on location, and being on location with him would be just like living with him," she replied miserably.

"But there'll be other people on the set."

Bridgette didn't want to tell Harry that when Adam was around his presence tended to blot out the existence of anyone else. "I don't see why they didn't keep their word and use Albee, the director originally assigned to the film," she said coolly. She resented being put in this position.

When she had begun divorce proceedings, Adam had made no attempt to contest—or even to contact her. Clearly his actions were an indication of how he really felt about her. Now she couldn't bear the idea of being near him. She had loved him so completely. *Had?* Who was she kidding? She still did, heaven help her. But she would never let him know that. After all, she had her pride . . . and her work.

"I told you," Harry said patiently, "Albee was just diagnosed as having acute appendicitis. He's in the hospital. Bridgette, honey, if you don't agree to play ball, you're going to find yourself labeled difficult to work with—and you know where that'll get you."

Yes, she knew. It didn't matter that she had several Academy Award nominations to her credit and that, except for the last picture, she had come up a winner every time. Studio heads had a way of remembering only the failures, never the successes. The people in charge of Bounty Studios were no different, especially now that they faced significant financial difficulties.

Bridgette sighed. "Okay, Harry, I'll do it," she conceded quietly.

"That's my girl," he said, beaming and patting her

back with obvious relief. "It won't be so bad. Trust me."

"It's not you I don't trust," she replied, gazing off into space.

Harry gave her a quick peck on the cheek and called out a cheery good-bye before Bridgette could change her mind.

Which she did—three times over the next two days, as she waited for Monday morning and the meeting with Adam to take place. They all had been asked to show up for the first reading of the script. Each time she considered the prospect of working closely with him, a warning signal went off inside her, telling her she was a fool to get near Adam again. But when she'd decide it would be better to back out, her fighting nature took over, calling her a coward and challenging her to put Adam in his place by showing him that she didn't care a fig about him.

The last time she had seen him had been when she'd burst into his trailer on the set of *No Love Lost* to tell him about her nomination by the Academy for best original screenplay. As far as Bridgette had been able to tell, not much love was being lost at that moment between Adam and the leading lady, Rhonda Farrell. Her flaming red hair trailing down her back and with very little else to cover her voluptuous body, Rhonda had her arms around Adam. There was smeared lipstick on his face. He appeared to be in the midst of a tryst.

Bridgette threw her wedding ring at the pair and let her hurt erupt in an explosion of accusations. Coming on the heels of hurt after hurt, this final insult had been the last straw.

She had started divorce proceedings the next day, in the heat of anger, and then felt too foolish to stop them.

Secretly, she hoped Adam would come storming back
into their now lonely house—she'd kicked him out the
same day she'd found him with Rhonda—and announce
loudly that he loved her and wasn't about to go through
any "damned divorce." She'd waited desperately for him
to tell her he really did love her, despite their recent
conflicts.

But he hadn't come. He hadn't called. He'd let the
divorce go through, and Bridgette had concluded that
she'd been a fool of the first degree to have ever gotten
involved with him.

But it hadn't always been that way, she thought three
days after her discussion with Harry, as she drove to the
studio and parked near lot 15. For a short time her life
had been wonderful.

She and Adam had met in New York at an awful off-
off Broadway play directed by Ralph, a mutual friend,
during Ralph's would-be director period. She and Adam
were two of the few people in the audience that opening
night, and they stayed up with Ralph to read the reviews,
which had been scathing. They significantly dampened
his ambitions to become a great director, but the world
of art probably wouldn't miss him, Bridgette and Adam
had decided after they'd put an inebriated Ralph to bed
and shared a cup of coffee in his tiny kitchen.

The cup of coffee had lasted until eight the next morning as they sat and talked the hours away. It was as if
an inner explosion had gone off inside Bridgette. Having
someone as utterly handsome and well-mannered as Adam
actually wanting to spend so much time with her made
something magical happen inside her. She found herself
opening up, telling him things she had never told another

living soul. She wanted to share with him her inner long-
ings and secret aspirations. Adam, in turn, had told her
about himself. Oh, it had taken a little prodding because
he was so terribly shy then—boyishly, charmingly shy—
but he'd shared many of his own feelings and dreams
that night, and by the time the morning sun was high in
the Manhattan sky, Bridgette felt as if they had known
each other forever.

She had fallen in love with him right then and there.
He had reached out to her...needed her. No one had
ever needed her before.

Her big break came first, through a friend of a friend
who introduced her to Harry. They met while he was in
New York on business. Harry read her work, liked it,
and urged her to turn her attention to screenplays, ex-
plaining that there was more of a market for them than
for the plays she was writing. She made her first sale
four months later. While celebrating the thrilling event,
Adam, more than a little emboldened by the wine they
were sharing, asked her to marry him. Bridgette accepted
with joyous alacrity.

At first they lived on love and dreams, and very little
money. But it was enough. Bridgette's work was going
well—she sold her second screenplay within three
months. Having grown more confident, she talked Adam
into quitting his job and moving to California, where she
set about putting him through film school.

Harry managed to place her work with increasing fre-
quency, while Adam became more and more involved
in producing student films at the University of Southern
California. One of his movies came to the attention of a
backer who owned a chain of movie theaters. The man
fancied that he saw something in the small, low-budget

film. He arranged to show the movie at one of his theaters and give Adam and his associates a small percentage of each evening's take. The movie attracted several film critics, who wrote very favorable reviews in the Los Angeles newspapers. Adam was launched.

From then on things happened too fast. Suddenly Bridgette hardly ever saw Adam. Several studios were vying for his time, and the pictures he worked on became larger and larger budget. Their life together took on the stereotyped trappings of the successful director with a vague wife in the background. At least that was the way Bridgette saw it. Starlets began phoning the house at all hours, asking for Adam, hoping to ingratiate themselves and get a big break in the movies. Bridgette got an un-listed phone number, and Adam's fans arrived in person instead—busloads of gawking, picture-snapping tour-ists; dauntless groupies, who waited for him outside the studio exit doors; and breathless ingenues who batted wide eyes and wiggled their hips. When Bridgette found a would-be starlet posing provocatively on their front lawn at five in the morning, dressed in the morning dew and very little else, she decided she'd had enough. They moved two weeks later.

But their address wasn't the only thing that changed. Adam changed, too. He was no longer the bashful boy from Iowa. He'd become a confident, forceful man who knew exactly what he wanted and how to get it. His screen successes had given him a sense of his own worth. He no longer needed Bridgette's encouragement, and he reveled in the attention that was showered upon him— the beautiful women who surrounded him, the demands to interview him, the red-carpet treatment he received wherever he went. At six foot two, he had both the stature and build of a blond god. And he was now one of the hottest directors around. It wasn't long before Bridgette realized that he was taking full advantage of *everything* offered to him and obviously enjoying it thoroughly. And that included whatever his female fans were willing to give. . . .

Olivia, their housekeeper, pointed out to Bridgette that Adam would have to be made of stone not to be at least slightly affected by all the attention, but her words didn't help Bridgette. She found herself slipping into the role of the shrewish wife, lashing out with words she didn't mean, in an attempt to cover her hurt at being left behind. Then Donna appeared on their doorstep.

It was obvious to Bridgette that her sister was only there to absorb some of the glamour that an association with a prominent Hollywood couple could generate. But Adam seemed quite taken with her, despite everything that Bridgette had once told him about how their parents had praised Donna's looks, talents, and abilities while ignoring Bridgette's. Nothing she had ever done had measured up to her older sister's accomplishments. In school they'd been compared constantly — with Bridgette found lacking. Her hurt was still a raw wound even after all these years, even after all the accomplishments and successes she'd garnered for herself.

Despite all this, Adam seemed to go out of his way to show Donna around, take her out to lunch, and be generally attentive to her while Bridgette was busy trying to meet a deadline. It broke Bridgette's heart. After everything she'd been denied because of Donna, she was now losing the one thing that mattered to her more than anything else in the world—her husband. And worst of all, Adam was falling hook, line, and sinker—without a struggle.

Bridgette was surprised when Donna returned to New York after a month's visit, but something in Bridgette's marriage had been broken beyond repair. Things were never the same again.

Remembering all this, Bridgette felt tears form as she headed toward the sound stage. She brushed them impatiently away with the back of her hand.

"Bridgette!"

She stopped, with her hand on the door that led to the sound stage, and turned toward Harry. He wasn't alone. Next to him stood Albert Davidson, a movie mogul cast in the old style.

The tall, distinguished looking, silver-maned man smiled down at Bridgette through a pencil-thin moustache.

She knew that the board viewed Davidson with less than a pleased eye. His first two "blockbusters" of the year had flopped miserably at the box office, and the studio had lost millions. It couldn't afford to foot the bill for another major setback. If that happened, a large purging would take place. Davidson's job was clearly on the line. He was here now to make sure things would go smoothly.

Bridgette squinted as they walked through the darkened studio, her eyes focusing on first one figure and then another. But not one of them was Adam.

Various people on the set hailed her and nodded deferentially toward Davidson. She was almost feeling at ease when they rounded a corner and she all but walked right into Adam's tall, muscular form. Bridgette backed off as her pulse began to beat madly. She struggled to keep her face expressionless.

Adam smiled down at her a little uncertainly, his green eyes warm and bright.

This was a big mistake, Bridgette's common sense told her. How she wished she could just walk away now while she still had a chance. The physical magic he made her feel was still there, as strong as ever. All she had to do was look at Adam and something inside her began to flower. She remembered the thrill of his first kiss, the wonder of the first time they made love. Steady, Bridgette, remember your pride, she told herself.

"Hello, Bridgette," Adam said, his voice soft and velvety, sending unbidden ripples over her skin. "How have you been?"

For one golden moment Bridgette remembered the shiver of anticipation she used to feel at the sound of his voice. After such a greeting he usually engulfed her in his strong arms, kissing her deeply and taking her on a sensual journey to ecstasy.

But her mental wanderings were aborted as she saw a honey-blond with a bountiful chest that strained against a wine-colored sweater take hold of Adam's arm and look at Bridgette with a knowing smirk. She was Sindee Allen, the screen's latest sex goddess, and Harry had told Bridgette just that morning that Sindee had been chosen to play the heroine instead of Bridgette's own choice for the part. The decision had not pleased her. It was her considered opinion that Sindee lacked a speck of talent, except for what the eye could see.

Bridgette considered herself fairly attractive, standing

about five foot four with everything rather well proportioned and in its proper place. Once, in a gossip column, she'd been described as having lively charm and an animated face, especially when she was making a point she believed in wholeheartedly. The article said her oval face was pretty, with expressive deep-set blue eyes and one flirtatious dimple that appeared whenever she laughed. Bridgette had read and reread the article when no one was looking. She didn't think she was at all beautiful, but it pleased her secretly that someone did. When Adam had called her beautiful, which he had often, she'd denied it adamantly, but her heart had always soared with pleasure.

She did know how to dress attractively. Today she had taken extra care, going through her wardrobe twice before deciding on a bone-white two-piece suit and a ruffled red silk blouse. Several heads turned as she passed by on her clicking four-inch heels, her legs peeking through the provocative front slit of her form-fitting skirt. But, standing next to Sindee Allen, Bridgette felt all her old insecurities return. She was no match for that *femme fatale*.

"I've been fine," Bridgette said icily, in answer to Adam's question. "And so have you from what I can see," she said, her eyes raking over Sindee's well-endowed form. Her own posture stiffened in response.

The warm light that had flickered briefly in Adam's eyes at the sight of her grew less bright. "Same old Bridgette," he said, shaking his head.

She didn't like his condescending tone. "Same old situation," she replied flippantly.

Harry stepped in quickly between them. "Er, why

don't we sit down and get on with the reading?" he suggested, looking nervously over his shoulder at Albert Davidson's disapproving expression.

"That sounds like a very good idea," Davidson said in a booming voice. "I know you two can work out your differences on your own time." He glanced from one to the other, and it seemed to Bridgette as if he was issuing an edict. "As a matter of fact," Davidson continued, looking directly at Bridgette, "I think it would be a good idea for you and Adam to get together over a nice candlelit dinner at the Brown Derby after the reading—on me."

"Thank you, but I like to choose my own company," Bridgette said crisply, paging through her copy of the script.

"You already have, Bridgette dear," Davidson said. "Shall we say around six? I'll send a studio car to pick you both up."

Bridgette felt what little control she had left slipping away. Harry squeezed her arm and led her to the center of the sound stage.

"Bridgette, you have to go along with the man," he said in a sharp whisper.

"Look, they bought my script, not my life for the next two months," she protested, suddenly terrified at the thought of being alone with Adam. "I've always cooperated with Davidson before. He's got nothing to complain about."

"He's got *plenty* to complain about," Harry insisted as they seated themselves at the long table. "The board is after his neck," he explained, glancing nervously over his shoulder and lowering his voice further. "He can't afford another flop—or even a picture that goes over budget. He wants everything to run smoothly. What happened yesterday doesn't count with the man. It's what you're doing for him this instant or intend to do in the future that matters. You should know that."

Yes, she did know that! She knew, too, that it didn't matter to Davidson that, since her divorce, she'd thrown herself into her job, working twice as hard as before, almost allowing the studio to dictate her life. By her own design, her life had become hectic. She got up at dawn to either write or to go off to some set to involve herself in the filming. She liked to keep a high profile.

Once, though, she had risen early in order to have more time with Adam. Then the wee hours of the morning had been filled with whispered words, sweet caresses, and wonderful lovemaking that seemed to last forever— but was over all too soon. A pang of regret twisted her heart. Damn! Why couldn't she learn to keep a tighter rein on her thoughts and emotions. All the memories she'd finally managed to forget were returning in full force, tumbling around as soon as she saw Adam. He looked better than he ever had. In fact, he looked perfect. A sigh escaped her lips, against her will.

In a gesture of concern, Harry patted her hand. Bridgette felt embarrassed. Was she that transparent? Were her feelings for Adam so evident to everyone? She resolved to keep herself in check. She refused to be an object of gossip—or worse yet, pity.

The table was filling up with the actors and actresses who had been cast to play roles in Bridgette's screenplay. They wore comfortable clothes, and looked to her more like a collection of would-be volleyball players than screen lovers who sent audiences sighing into their pillows at night. An array of ragged T-shirts, paint-splattered jeans, and cut-offs met Bridgette's eyes. The stuff that dreams are made out of, she thought wryly.

Her gaze drifted to Adam's corner of the room, where he was deep in conversation with Sindee, whose eyes were smoldering with what appeared to be passion. The starlet seemed to do justice to the first part of her name— sin, thought Bridgette.

Adam's sea-green eyes looked over the heads of the others and met Bridgette's stare. He winked at her before she had a chance to turn away.

A tight knot of apprehension—and desire—formed in the pit of her stomach. What was she getting herself into?

2

THE SCRIPT READING went well, at first. Everyone seemed more or less content with the script—until Adam began to point out difficulties with several of the scenes. Bridgette's eyes narrowed as she listened to him pull apart bits of dialogue she had slaved over for hours.

"Here," Adam said, flipping pages of the script, "in Scene 85, the heroine comes off looking like a witch. This isn't the kind of woman the hero would risk his neck for, taking on countless warring Saracens to bring her back to the safety of his tent. Just look at the way she treats him in this scene." He pointed to several lines. "A woman in love shouldn't sound like a shrew," he added, turning his magnetic eyes to Bridgette.

That was all she needed.

15

"Perhaps, if the woman in love is given enough reason, she'll sound like a shrew," she pointed out, sharply stinging from his remark.

"But there wasn't any reason," he retorted in a calm voice.

"Are we talking about the same script?" asked one of the actors, trying to find his place. He glanced at Adam's page.

Bridgette retreated, somewhat chagrined but not showing it. *"I* was," she said coolly. "I'm not sure what Mr. Reeves was talking about."

"Then read your own script," Adam advised mildly. "I'm talking about the success or failure of a movie. Your story lacks consistency."

"Mr. Davidson likes it." Bridgette rose to face Adam, who had moved to the seat opposite her at the long table.

He rose, too, and for a moment they stared face to face. "I didn't say it wasn't a good story," Adam said. "I said it needed tightening and reworking. Surely you can handle that. After all, your imagination is so over-developed there should be room for a few more fabrications," he said pointedly. "There always was before."

Nothing had changed between them. Adam still managed to incense her within a minute, just like he had repeatedly in the months before their divorce.

Silence fell as all eyes turned toward them. Davidson apparently decided that it would be prudent to dismiss the rest of the cast, which he did, leaving Adam and Bridgette alone with only Harry and himself as buffers. As Davidson drew himself up, Bridgette stifled an impulse to leave with the others.

Davidson cleared his throat imperially. "Before a picture gets started there's bound to be a little tension. I want that resolved," he said, his eyes darting from Bridgette to Adam. "Now you, Reeves, direct a good picture. And you, Ms. Santaniello, write a good screenplay—or did until recently." Bridgette curbed her anger at his comment. "There's no reason for tension, do you understand?" Davidson stated in a commanding voice.

As if it could all be resolved just like that, Bridgette thought bitterly. What right did he have to act high and mighty when he knew that the tension had nothing to do with the picture? But, in the interests of her career and because Harry was eyeing her nervously, she held her tongue. Saying something now wouldn't solve anything. She was doomed to work on this movie with Adam, and that was that. She'd just have to make the best of it.

Davidson's face softened slightly. "That's better. Now I trust the two of you will have a pleasant dinner."

"Oh, I just remembered," Bridgette broke in. "I have a previous engagement." She rose to leave. After all, her personal life was her own.

"Break it," Davidson barked. Giving them all a last baleful glance, he left, taking Harry with him.

Bridgette was alone with Adam, alone on a suddenly darkened sound stage. She felt vastly uncomfortable now as she realized how closely Adam was regarding her, sitting in his chair and looking at her with eyes that still melted her resistance.

"You've lost weight," he said finally.

She shrugged. "Olivia doesn't cook well," she said of her housekeeper.

"I remember." Adam nodded. "But you could."

"I don't like cooking for one person." She began to

edge toward the door. She hated the fact that he made her nervous. There was a time when he didn't. Then all the tingly butterflies had been wonderfully delicious. Now she felt acutely self-conscious.

"Then there's no one in your life?" he asked bluntly.

There wasn't, but she'd die before she'd admit as much to him. For a long time after the divorce—finalized almost a year ago—every time she had opened a gossip column there had been pictures of Adam with a new girl on his arm. It seemed as if he was making up for lost time. But recently his name had been noticeably absent, which made Bridgette wonder if someone special had turned up, someone he didn't want to share with photographers, someone he took to private places like the ones they had once gone to. She couldn't let him know that she spent many nights alone, reading or trying not to remember the past, when things had been different.

She didn't want to go out. Going out meant getting involved in new relationships and running the risk of being hurt again. She hadn't fully recovered from the wounds she had already acquired. Perhaps she never would.

"You don't expect me to cook for my dates, do you?" she asked with a little laugh.

Adam looked at her thoughtfully. "You always laughed like that when you were lying," he said.

She regarded him testily and refused to reply to his comment. "If you'll excuse me, I have to . . . meet someone for lunch," she said, happy with the excuse she'd just thought of.

"See you at dinner," he called after her, making no move to follow her.

She spun around. "You don't mean you're really going

to listen to Davidson, do you? We can just tell him we went out. We don't really have to do it."

"I make it a point always to listen to the head of the studio," Adam replied innocently, but even at that distance Bridgette could see the twinkle in his eyes. He was up to something, she'd stake her life on it. "Besides, there's the car," he said. "What would we tell the chauffeur? See, Bridge, you keep forgetting loose ends. That's always been your problem."

She said nothing as she turned away and hurried out the door. Her problem, she decided, was having fallen in love with an overwhelmingly handsome man and never having gotten over it.

Once in her car, her seat belt buckled, she flipped on her tape deck and filled the interior of her silver-blue Mercedes with songs from the musicals of the forties. Usually music helped soothe her and propel her into a relaxed, creative mood in which she could forget reality and leave its trials and tribulations far behind. Today, however, it only reminded her of the late-night movies she and Adam had watched in their one-room studio apartment in New York, sharing popcorn they'd made on their tiny stove. Adam. Everywhere she turned, Adam.

She switched off the tape deck and turned on the radio, hoping the loud, dissonant contemporary sounds would chase away the blues. But her inner frustration, combined with the fast rhythms of the music, caused her to drive exceedingly fast up the winding road. She narrowly missed an oncoming car and, as if in a haze, just kept on going. A policeman flashed his lights and forced her to pull over to the side of the road, where he gave her a ticket for her negligence. It did absolutely nothing for her mood, which was thoroughly black by the time she arrived home.

Bridgette slammed the front door, jarring the vase on the foyer table and sending an echo reverberating through the house.

"Another perfect session?" Olivia asked dryly. Olivia wasn't one of those good little housekeepers who faded into the background when her work was done. She was more of a housekeeper in the tradition of the Thelma Ritter roles in the fifties, which was probably why, Bridgette decided, she kept her around. Olivia's version of cleaning house would bring the editors of *House Beautiful* to tears, and Julia Child would stamp CENSORED on Olivia's forehead after watching her in the kitchen and sampling the results. But Olivia, a peppery, short, redheaded woman whose age was a mystery to Bridgette, had grown on her. Bridgette even forgave Olivia her partiality toward Adam.

"It was awful," Bridgette moaned, heading for her favorite armchair, which clashed with the decor of the sunny, uncluttered living room with its off-white walls and beige furniture. The chair was deep brown and covered with fur that had seen better days. It was the first piece of furniture she and Adam had bought at a regular furniture store instead of from a secondhand dealer. Although she had thrown out almost every other article that had reminded her of her life with him, Bridgette had kept the chair because it was comfortable, or so she told herself.

Olivia hated it. "Someday that thing is either going to absorb you, kid, or break right out from under you," Olivia told her, eyeing the chair disdainfully.

"We'll talk about it then, okay?" Bridgette replied raising a hand to her forehead.

"You sick?" Olivia asked, peering at her with motherly concern. Whenever Bridgette became ill, Olivia's finer instincts rose to the surface, and she kept her quips and drier comments to herself until Bridgette was well enough to handle them.

"I'm working on getting sick," Bridgette said, her head really pounding. She waved the traffic ticket she had just received under Olivia's nose. The older woman took it from her.

"You autographing these things nowadays?" Olivia asked sarcastically, handing the ticket back to Bridgette.

"That was just the *end* of my day. That wasn't even the main event." Bridgette heaved a deep sigh and put her feet up on the ottoman.

"So how did the first session go?" Olivia prompted, pushing Bridgette's feet to one side and sitting down.

"Straight out of a horror movie."

"Davidson his natural, charming self?" Oliver asked.

"Worse," Bridgette mumbled, closing her eyes as she tried to forget the scene. Scene. How many scenes was Adam going to make her rewrite out of pure spite? That's all it was, just spite.

"You going to volunteer any information, or do I have to run down your throat and pull it all out, bit by bit?" Oliva demanded.

"You're waiting for me to tell you about Adam, aren't you?" Bridgette said, annoyed.

"In a word, yes."

"He's just as terrible as ever." Bridgette slid further down into the chair.

"In other words, you've still got that old feeling for him, don't you?" Olivia sounded thoroughly content with the situation. Even though Bridgette's eyes were closed, she could tell Olivia was beaming.

Bridgette bolted upright and her eyes shot open. "I do not!" she cried.

Olivia smiled as if she knew better. "I saw a picture of him recently. He's still a hunk."

"He's still an insensitive boor," Bridgette shot back.

"That's not what all his awards say," Olivia replied with a smug look as she rose and headed for the kitchen. "Well, I guess I'd better get back to work. We're having pot roast tonight."

"I won't be eating here."

Olivia retraced her steps. "You got a date?" she asked incredulously.

"I'm going out to eat with someone," Bridgette hedged. "Davidson's orders."

"Who?"

"I had to answer less questions for my mother," Bridgette protested, not enjoying any of this.

"Who?" Olivia repeated.

"Adam," Bridgette mumbled, looking away from Olivia to the design on the white marble fireplace. The frieze depicted a nymph being seduced by a young god, who looked just like Adam. Oh Lord, was she losing her mind?

"Adam!" Olivia exclaimed. Bridgette looked back at her. A twisted smile was on Olivia's thin lips, exposing a mouthful of crooked teeth.

Bridgette glared at her. "Yes, Adam. But you needn't sound so happy. Davidson ordered us to bury the hatchet over dinner. I'll be civil," she promised with a careless shrug.

"I'll be gone," Olivia announced with gleeful determination.

"You'll be what!" Bridgette sat at rigid attention, her defenses on full alert.

"I'll leave you a clear field," Olivia promised. "I can stay with my sister for the night—for the week, if you want," she offered.

"You'll do no such thing," Bridgette ordered, rising. "You're not leaving me alone with that man." Further words failed her.

Olivia looked disappointed. "You always were hard-headed."

Bridgette looked her housekeeper straight in the eye. "Olivia, did it ever occur to you that as my housekeeper you're not supposed to criticize me?"

"Nope," Olivia said pertly and she left the room.

Bridgette shook her head wearily and went in search of two aspirins. If she was lucky, she'd be the first person to die of a headache—before six that evening.

Six o'clock was approaching on what seemed like winged feet. Bridgette had already spent hours trying to figure out what to wear, wavering between a suit of armor and a nearly breakaway dress.

At five Olivia came in to check on her. "Just thought you might need a little help," she said, entering without an invitation.

Bridgette stood wrapped in her blue robe, in front of the closet. She had been standing there for twenty minutes. Olivia made a beeline for her wardrobe.

"Olivia, I'm perfectly capable of dressing myself," Bridgette protested tartly, her nerves on edge.

"Ordinarily, maybe," Olivia conceded. It was clear she didn't consider tonight ordinary.

Bridgette sighed and plopped down on the bed. There was no harm in seeing what Olivia came up with.

But perhaps there *was* harm, Bridgette decided when Olivia pulled out a hot-pink dress that dipped provocatively at the neckline and rose up at the middle of the hemline in an inviting front part. Olivia indicated a silver-gray belt with matching shoes to complete the outfit.

"There," she said, laying the dress on the bed next to Bridgette. "Wear that. And don't forget your push-up bra."

"Olivia!" Bridgette exclaimed between clenched teeth. "You sound like you're preparing a call girl for a busy night's work! You should have been a madam."

"I should have been a governess for your children by now," Olivia corrected. "I like little kids better than dirty dishes and dusting."

"There are diapers, you know," Bridgette reminded her archly.

Olivia shrugged. "Should be no reason why you wouldn't pitch in as well. It'd be your kid."

"I could have children with someone other than Adam," Bridgette pointed out, trying not to lose her temper.

Olivia regarded her closely for a long moment. "After you've had filet mignon, why would you settle for plain hamburger?"

Bridgette bit her lip. "Why don't you go and start an Adam Reeves fan club and leave me alone?" she cried.

"Because you're the one who's responsible for the divorce," Olivia said quietly.

"I'm the one!" Bridgette felt her eyes popping wide. "I'm not the one who ran around with bleached-blond fluffs."

"He didn't run around with any such thing. Look, he

got a little carried away with success, that's all. You married a man, not a wooden dummy."

"I married a man who promised to be faithful."

"Just because he flirted a little and drank up a bit of what those women were dishing out doesn't prove he was unfaithful. I never saw him being unfaithful to you," Olivia said firmly.

"It's not the kind of thing a person sells tickets to," Bridgette retorted.

Olivia merely shook her head and left the room.

Besides, Bridgette thought, Adam knew how uncertain she was about her ability to hold onto him. How could he have flaunted all those women in front of her. They were all so much prettier than she was. Hollywood was full of beautiful women. They should never have come to California. Moving there had been like signing her own death warrant. As soon as he'd become successful, Adam had ceased to need her advice and encouragement. What did he want with her when all those generously endowed women were throwing themselves at him?

Bridgette slipped into the pink dress and tugged at the zipper behind her. She missed having Adam pull up her zippers. More than that, she missed having him pull down her zippers. . . .

Stop it, Bridgette, she told her reflection in the mirror, you're letting Olivia get to you.

But it wasn't Olivia who was getting to her and it wasn't Olivia she was afraid of when the doorbell chimed melodically.

"Mr. Reeves, welcome back!"

Olivia's enthusiastic voice reached Bridgette's ears as she turned down the long hallway to the foyer. Olivia made Adam's arrival sound like a homecoming.

"Don't sound so elated, Olivia, he's only here by edict of the big boss," Bridgette remarked dryly as she walked into the foyer.

Her heart stopped.

Adam stood in her living room doorway, looking larger than life. He wore a light-blue suit with a dark-blue shirt that made him look more handsome than any man had a right to look. Bridgette couldn't slow her racing pulse or quiet the ache of desire that throbbed deep inside her.

All at once she realized that she *could* have refused this date and undoubtedly *should* have. But some part of her had chosen to play the devil's advocate. Some part of her wanted this meeting with Adam, away from the studio, away from the curious eyes of strangers who'd had no part in their life together before Hollywood. She was a fool, she told herself.

Adam smiled at her and her insides seemed to melt. "Very nice dress."

"I picked it out," Olivia piped up proudly.

"Thank you, Olivia," Adam said, his twinkling eyes never leaving Bridgette's face, which made her tremble.

"I'll be going to my sister's now," Olivia announced loudly. "Remember, I'll be staying overnight, so there won't be anyone here to get your breakfast," she told Bridgette. But her eyes were on Adam.

Bridgette's cheeks flushed hot.

"I think you've gotten her angry," Adam stage-whispered to Olivia.

He was laughing at her, Bridgette knew. He probably thought she had put Olivia up to it. She had a good mind not to go with him after all. No, on second thought, she'd go all right, and show that big oaf that all his so-called charm left her cold. After all, she knew it was only a façade. The wonderful, sensitive man who had been Adam was gone.

"Shall we?" he asked, holding out his elbow for her to take.

"Well, at least you've still got good manners," Bridgette remarked dryly.

"A lot of the other old things haven't changed either," he told her, holding her gaze.

Bridgette's eyes wavered. Why did he have to be so damn attractive?

Without another word, Adam led her toward the black limousine that was parked in front of the house. He opened the car door for her and helped her inside. She had almost forgotten what such consideration was like, she thought as he got in after her and slid ever so close.

"Okay, Peters, you know the way," Adam told the chauffeur, who closed the door after him and seated himself in front, discreetly closing the black curtain that separated him from the passengers.

All at once a wave of panic washed over Bridgette. She was alone with Adam, and she felt very much at his mercy.

3

"THE EVENING MIGHT go better if you'd take that angry scowl off your face," Adam said cheerfully.

Bridgette stared straight ahead at the black velvet curtain that isolated them in a small world where her common sense told her she shouldn't be. "I'm not scowling," she told Adam tersely.

He leaned over as if to whisper a confidence to her, his warm breath caressing her face and reviving a thousand sweet memories, none of which she wanted to recall just then. Perhaps not ever.

"Then I hate to be the one to tell you this," Adam said, "but someone obviously hijacked your face and has taken it over. There's a terrible scowl sitting on it. Hardly even looks like you. It'll give you wrinkles."

Embarrassed, annoyed, and slightly amused despite herself Bridgette let the look fade into a half smile.

Adam nodded his approval. "Needs work," he told her, "but it's a good beginning."

"There isn't going to be a beginning," Bridgette told him, wiping the smile from her face, clenching her hands in her lap and staring out the window as the car wound down to the heart of Rodeo Drive.

"Well, I'd hate to think I put on a new suit for a continuation of this afternoon's session," Adam said with a laugh. He reached for her hand, his strong fingers unbending her fingers with ease. Bridgette felt a warm ache surge inside her as he clasped her hand in his.

She turned, ready to say something to maintain the protective barrier between them, but the sight of him looking at her with a light in his eyes that used to be for her alone made the words die in her throat.

"How about a truce?" he suggested softly.

Bridgette bit the inside of her lip, as if considering his words. "We're both grown-ups," she replied coolly. "We can act in a civil fashion."

"I don't have to act," Adam told her, then flashed her a boyish grin that seemed to light up his face.

He always did have a heart-melting smile, she thought. In the beginning it had ended many of their arguments and become a prelude to lovemaking. For a while she'd feel secure in his love—until the next young thing wiggled into his life, batting overly made-up eyes and sighing breathlessly. And then, when he had paid all that attention to Donna, knowing how Bridgette felt about her older sister, Bridgette had been hurt to the quick. Her feelings had meant nothing to him then and meant even less to him now.

The car came to a stop, and the chauffeur opened the door for them. Adam emerged first and took Bridgette's hand rather than her elbow.

Since her divorce, Bridgette hadn't dated even one of the eligible men who'd asked her, and she'd quickly gained a reputation for being all work and no play. Good-looking men and not-so-good-looking men went on to seek more eager partners while she spent her nights with a typewriter, listening to Olivia berate her for staying home, on the one hand, and for sending Adam away, on the other. For the award dinners and other events that required an escort, Bridgette would either tell Harry he was taking her or ask a producer or director, all of whom were either happily married and willing to do her a favor, or much older and firmly entrenched in bachelorhood. To them Bridgette was one of the guys.

But the touch of Adam's hand as he led her toward the restaurant brought back memories of their long walks on Fifth Avenue, when they could ill afford any type of date other than window shopping. She remembered, too, all the hours they'd spent in the Museum of Natural History, not really seeing any of the exhibits, just talking, oblivious to the passing crowds.

Why, why had things changed for them? Perhaps if Adam hadn't been so good-looking she wouldn't have worried so much.

She beat back the thought with sheer will power. Things had changed because the successes they'd dreamed about had taken a toll on their lives. Adam just didn't know how to accept the praise people had heaped on him.

Even now as they walked into the elegant restaurant several people greeted them, mostly women who smiled broadly at Adam. Their glances did not include Bridgette.

"Admiring fans even here," she said sarcastically as they passed a well-dressed blonde whose eyes sparkled as they followed Adam.

Noting the direction of Bridgette's gaze, Adam said, "I could throw a bag over my head and have you lead me in, but that doesn't quite cut a suave image."

"And you're very concerned with a suave image, aren't you?" she replied as the mâitre d' seated her. She felt her worst side coming out. Oh, why couldn't she stop caring?

Adam leaned forward, his chin cupped in his palm. "You were the one who said she'd change me over from an Iowa hayseed, remember?"

"I did too good a job," Bridgette replied almost sadly, hiding behind her menu and pretending to consider the selections.

A waiter came over to their table, a bright, fixed smile on his face. "Would you care for some wine, Mr. Reeves?"

At the mention of his name, Adam looked up and cast a long glance at the young man. It was obvious to Bridgette that the waiter was waiting for his big acting break— not unlike a quarter of the population of Southern California.

Adam smiled his patient, professional smile. "You know who I am," he said, leaving the conversation open.

Well, at least Adam was not a snob, Bridgette thought grudgingly. He had always said that if he ever made it, he'd listen as patiently as he could to every hopeful who came his way. If only so many of them hadn't been women. . . .

"Doesn't everyone know who you are?" the young man asked enthusiastically.

An amused smile creased Adam's rugged face. "Are you an actor?" he asked pleasantly.

"I've done a couple of horror movies and been in a few crowd scenes," the young man replied eagerly, looking hopeful as he stood a little straighter and tilted his head, probably to show what he must think was his best side, Bridgette thought, hiding a smile.

Adam seemed to be considering an idea. He turned to Bridgette. "How about that young page who dies helping the hero save the princess?" he said. "Doesn't this young man fit the description?"

"Roland?" Bridgette asked in surprise, recalling the character he meant. What was Adam up to?

"That's the one," he said, nodding. He glanced back at the waiter, who seemed to be hanging on Adam's every word.

"But that role's been cast," Bridgette pointed out.

"Bret Hasting's agent called up this afternoon and said he wanted more money for his client or no go. Bret's having delusions of grandeur these days, so I said no."

Bridgette shrugged. They didn't even know if the waiter could act, but he certainly did look like what she had in mind. "You're the director," she said. The waiter smiled at her broadly.

"Yes, but you're so fussy about your casting," Adam reminded her. She didn't know whether the comment was meant to sting, but it did, despite Adam's mild expression.

"It's okay with me," she said disinterestedly.

Adam reached into his pocket, pulled out a card, and scribbled instructions on the back of it. "Here," he said, handing it to the ecstatic young man. "Present this to the front guard at Bounty Studios and ask him to point you toward Sound Stage 15. I'll have a test set up for you by morning."

"Thank you, thank you, Mr. Reeves, thank you." An expression of euphoric disbelief covered the waiter's handsome features. "What can I ever do to..."

"You could try taking our order," Adam said with a grin.

"Oh, sure, sure," the waiter said, reaching into his pocket for his pad and pencil, missing them the first try, then smiling foolishly as he succeeded on his second attempt.

Adam ordered for himself, then went on to order for Bridgette before she could even open her mouth. The waiter took away their menus, almost bowing as he left.

"You didn't even ask me what I want," Bridgette accused Adam.

"I know what you want," he told her with a smile that indicated he was referring to more than just dinner.

"My tastes might have changed," she told him indignantly.

He looked at her for a long, long moment, his eyes caressing her. "I don't think so," he said softly.

Disturbed by his words, Bridgette lowered her eyes and tried to change the subject. "That was a nice thing you did for that boy," she said.

"I am nice, remember?"

She spread her napkin carefully on her lap. "I remember very little," she said vaguely, her voice cold.

"I remember everything," Adam told her, his voice low and husky.

Bridgette took a deep breath, determined to keep the

conversation on a professional level. "The boy looks like he's going to fall all over himself on the set tomorrow."

"If he does, he won't make the test. But I have a feeling he'll come through," Adam told her. His smile of amusement deepened. "You keep calling him a boy. He looks older than you are. Have you gotten to feel so old?" he asked, never taking his eyes off her.

"No," she said with a toss of her head, "just more mature."

"Oh." She knew he was grinning at her—laughing at her the way he had in the beginning to get her out of her serious moods, when her stories didn't sell and she was sure she had no talent.

The waiter returned with the wine. "My name's Barret," he said formally, as if remembering that he hadn't told his idol this piece of information. "Barret Browning."

Bridgette winced.

"Is it now?" Adam asked, waiting.

"No," the waiter admitted, turning red. "It's Joel Sommers."

"Much better," Adam told him.

Joel withdrew, beaming.

"You keep this up and all the hopefuls are going to call you Saint Adam," Bridgette said, sipping her wine.

"I've been called worse things," Adam replied. "By you as I remember it."

"Can't we keep the past out of it?" Bridgette asked uncomfortably. "You just did a good deed akin to the fishes and the loaves for that boy—man," she corrected herself, refusing to look at Adam. "Can't you just bask in that?"

"How can I keep the past out of this?" Adam asked

seriously. "Every time I look at you I remember the past—the walks, the dreams, the kisses. Remember the kisses?" he teased fondly, leaning closer.

"How can you remember mine amid all the others you gave out?" she demanded, feeling some of her old fire as she challenged him.

"Still the scissor-tongued wonder," he said almost sadly, shaking his head. "Bridgette," he whispered, "what happened to us?"

Though his words tore at her heart, she rolled her eyes in exasperation. "Oh, please, Adam, I wrote better lines than that in the eighth grade." She wanted desperately to end that line of conversation.

Adam waited while Joel set down their appetizers and withdrew before he continued. "I'm not writing lines," he said earnestly. "I'm asking you a question."

"Well, you ought to know," she retorted. "I could never find you amid the crowd of women that surrounded you." Her tone was bitter.

He looked genuinely annoyed and seemed to struggle with his temper. "I could always find *you*," he told her. "You were always scowling."

Bridgette pressed her lips together. *"That's* what happened to us." She jabbed at her food, then looked up accusingly. "Do you think it was easy being married to someone who was prettier than me?"

Adam looked at her as if she was crazy. "What did Joel put in your drink?" he asked, picking up the long-stemmed goblet and peering inside.

She grabbed the glass back. "You *were* beautiful. The girls were beautiful—and I was on the sidelines, a runner-up."

Adam shook his head. "Bridgette, you're talking nonsense. Why are you so unsure of yourself? Why must you imagine I was involved with a score of women?"

"Oh, so now I'm hallucinating," she retorted, incensed. "I suppose I hallucinated that semi-nude girl on our lawn, too."

Adam laughed. "No, she was real, all right. I don't know how she got over that brick wall—"

"The Easter Bunny brought her as a surprise," Bridgette supplied dryly, pushing away her fruit cocktail after having taken three bites.

"That's why you're getting so skinny," Adam observed. "You don't eat enough."

"I don't eat when I've lost my appetite," she retorted, rising, fully intending to leave. She didn't want to rip open old wounds, especially not those to do with Adam. And certainly not while he was watching her with eyes that seemed to look straight into her soul.

He put his hand over hers, stopping her flight. "How about the truce we declared?" he asked, his voice soft once more.

"Great White Director spoke with forked tongue," she said, looking down at him. From whatever angle she looked, he was still gorgeous. She could see why women were always after him, throwing themselves at him even when he had no jobs to offer them, even though he wasn't really the soft-hearted fool he seemed just then, she thought, angry tears welling up in her eyes. She wasn't even still sure she knew what she was angry about— their failed marriage, his infidelity, or the memories that kept attacking her.

"Great White Director will try again," he told her patiently, not releasing her hand. "If you want, we'll talk about the picture or the weather or whether Shakespeare's mother went to bed with Francis Bacon. Anything you want, as long as it won't set off your short fuse."

"I don't have a short fuse," she snapped.

"And then there was the story about the three bears," he said lightly. "Bridgette, when our friends used to call you Li'l Miss Dynamite they weren't suggesting that you were only six inches tall," he said with a grin.

She had to laugh at that.

Adam sighed and looked relieved. "Sit?"

She nodded slowly.

Adam's smile seeped into every corner of her being, and for a moment she relaxed.

"There're no lights on," Adam observed as the limousine stopped in front of Bridgette's house. Their house once, she thought.

She glanced out the window over his broad shoulder, touching it for an instant before snatching back her hand as if she had touched a hot coal.

"Oh well, Olivia's probably gone to bed," she said nervously.

"She said she was going out," Adam replied, studying her.

"So?" she said uncomfortably, beginning to panic. He was going to invite himself in, and if Olivia had gone through with her threat and left, Bridgette definitely didn't want him in the house.

"So there've been a lot of robberies in the area and there might be a burglar hiding in there now, lying in wait in the shadows," Adam told her, helping her out of the car. He stood very close to her and looked down into her face. "I'd be worried about you."

"I'm from the Bronx, remember?" she said. "I can take care of myself."

"Then maybe it's the burglar I should be worried about," he retorted dryly.

"There is no burglar," she insisted, though alarm bells seemed to be going off inside her head.

"Let's check to make sure," he insisted, going up the stone path leading to the front door.

"Adam, go home," Bridgette ordered, but her words fell on deaf ears. He held out his hand, waiting for the key. She slapped it into his hand. He merely grinned, then opened the door.

Bridgette squared her shoulders and marched past him, hoping fervently that Olivia was hiding in some corner, waiting to get a glimpse of Adam.

But she was nowhere in sight, at least not in the foyer or the living room. Bridgette turned to Adam. "See, no burglar. Now go home."

"This was home once," he reminded her.

"Go to your new home," she emphasized.

He shook his head. "I haven't finished checking yet."

Bridgette threw up her hands in despair and followed as Adam went from room to room.

"You really don't have to do this. That poor man," she said, gesturing in the general direction of the chauffeur who was waiting in the parked limousine, "wants to go home to his wife and kids."

"He's a bachelor," Adam said as he walked through the wide country kitchen and attached family room. "A little rest will do him good." He winked at Bridgette, who clenched her fists.

The next room they came to was Bridgette's bedroom.

"Ah, what have we here?" he asked dramatically, opening the door. "A bedroom."

Bridgette crossed her arms in front of her chest. "Yes, oddly enough," she said testily, "I left the rooms in the same place they were before you left—"

"Was thrown out," Adam corrected without skipping a beat.

"You didn't try to contest it."

"At the time, I was tired of the accusations and decided to live up to the image you had cast for me," he said, opening her walk-in closet. "You did change the room, though," he said, observing the decor.

He turned toward the king-size canopied bed. The curtains that hung about it were mocha colored with light-blue butterflies that floated delicately on the background, matching the bedspread, sham, and throw pillows.

"The brass bed's gone."

"I never liked brass."

"I didn't know that," he said, surprised. He sat down on the bed. "I like it," he said, patting the mattress.

"I'm sure the decorator will be thrilled," Bridgette replied, standing as if rooted to the carpet.

"Looks kind of lonely though," Adam commented, looking back down on the bed. "I don't remember your needing this much room to sleep." He looked up at her, his eyes soft. "You used to kind of curl up like a contented kitten, fitting in right here," he said, gesturing to the front of his torso. His eyes searched hers.

"Could we curtail our trip down memory lane, please? There's no burglar here. There's no one here except you. Now could we get this over with? You've fulfilled Davidson's orders. He'll be very happy with you," she said, turning on her heel and walking out the door, to the living room.

She had to get away from the bed, before panic set in. She knew her limits, and she wasn't about to give that oaf the satisfaction of knowing that, yes, she'd still love to be in his arms. If only things were that simple...

"I didn't come to please Davidson," Adam said, striding quickly to catch up with her.

"Oh? Then why did you do it?" she asked coolly.

"For the same reason you did." He knowingly looked at her. She flushed for a moment, then almost clenched her teeth together.

"I came to keep Harry from having a coronary. I thought I owed it to him." She ignored a pang of guilt at her half-lie.

Adam stepped forward and slipped his hands around her waist as he looked down at her, holding her fast with his eyes. "And what do you owe me?" he whispered.

"Not a thing," she tried to snap, but her voice trembled.

The lights of the living room seemed to wink madly as if a cloud had suddenly surrounded her. Adam bent his head and pulled her close. Slowly his lips descended, touching hers gently but sending a reaction of megaton strength rocketing through her body. Her nerves were frayed. That's why she was feeling like this. Her suddenly weak hands tried to push him away before she was totally engulfed, but it was too late. His kiss had claimed her, pushing her over the brink into the hot, blinding land Adam's kisses had always taken her to. Her head swirled as blasts of heat consumed her, separating her from her mortal body and setting her adrift in a world of bright colors that alternated with hot, black abysses. She wanted him. After all these months, she wanted him desperately. She had known it all along. Damn him!

His very touch set her on fire. Though her head was spinning, she was aware that his hands were not idle. His fingers had slipped under her clothes and were exploring the swell of her breasts, exploring curves and planes he'd once known well. Ever so slowly his hands swept along her silky skin, branding her as his own, reminding her how much she still belonged to him.

"That dress has been driving me crazy all night," he whispered huskily.

His words aroused her from the unreal world she'd entered. With all the strength that had served her well in the years she had struggled to make a name for herself, Bridgette pushed him back. "Satisfied?" she asked bitterly.

"Oh, I wouldn't say that just yet," he replied softly, meaningfully.

Bridgette's eyes narrowed. "That's all you'll get, Mr. Reeves. I haven't sat here for eleven months just waiting for you to come back to me."

Adam looked at her for a long moment, as if searching for the truth. "You know, Bridgette, your creative talents are exceptional, but they're sometimes a liability more than an asset."

"What are you talking about?" she demanded hotly, making sure there was more than a little space between them.

"You keep imagining scenarios in which you're the ugly duckling and I'm the rake. Neither is true, yet you let it ruin our life together."

"I don't think I made up anything," she said, raising her chin defiantly.

Despite her protests, Adam pulled her into his arms, his strong hands keeping her in place. But this time he made no move to kiss her.

"If you're going to wrestle with me..." she threatened.

"No, Bridgette, I'm just going to open your eyes and put you in your place," he said, finally releasing her.

"You and what army?" she shot back, then was immediately chagrined. She sounded like an adolescent.

"Oh, please, Bridgette, I was writing better lines than that in the ninth grade," Adam said, mimicking her.

"No, *eighth* grade," she corrected, allowing herself a half-smile.

Adam nodded, apparently accepting the left-hand apology. He looked at her with steady eyes, then headed for the door. "You know, Bridge, we're going to be spending a lot of time together in the next few weeks." He smiled. "Not much to do in the Great Salt Lake Desert." His eyes twinkled mischievously as he closed the door behind him, his voice holding unspoken promises.

4

"I ASSUME IT didn't go well," Olivia said the next morning as Bridgette entered the daffodil-yellow kitchen. She had spent a sleepless night, trying vainly to keep thoughts of Adam out of her head, and now she gave Olivia a bleary look as she sank down in a chair at the kitchen table. "What makes you say that?" she muttered.

"I heard you tossing and turning all night," Olivia said. "And even if I hadn't, one look at you tells me that you put in a hell of a night—by yourself," she added accusingly.

"Let's not go into that again," Bridgette said wearily. She took a sip of hot coffee and sighed. Suddenly a new thought occurred to her. "I thought you were going to stay at your sister's." She watched Olivia move about the bright kitchen, making breakfast.

"My sister was up to her ears in two kids with the chicken pox, so I went to the movies instead." She stood poised with an egg-covered fork in her hand. "You know, that last movie of yours"—she wiggled the fork from side to side—"was just so-so."

Bridgette arched her left brow. "Oh? And just what about it did not meet your high standards, Madame Critic?" she asked playfully.

"Not enough romance," Olivia told her, pulling an errant egg shell out of the bowl. "But I guess you can't be expected to write about what you don't know," she added with a pitying glance.

"And maybe you shouldn't talk about what *you* don't know," Bridgette countered testily, getting up to pour herself another cup of coffee.

Olivia smiled wickedly. "Oh, I've had plenty of romance in my time. I could tell *you* a thing or two." She winked and sighed.

Bridgette waved away the start of a long story as she took a sip of her coffee. "Not interested at the moment, Olivia. I've got to get ready for my flight." But she made no move to go. She wished she could linger here forever. Anything not to see Adam again.

"To or from?" Olivia asked.

Bridgette caught her meaning immediately. "I am going *to* Utah, God help me. I have never fled *from* anything in my life."

"Huh!" Olivia vigorously mixed the eggs, tossing in plain bread crumbs with a heavy hand, then reaching for the milk. An array of seasonings that Bridgette knew could easily turn her strong stomach to jelly surrounded the bowl. Bridgette figured it was time to leave.

"You," she said, draining the last drop of fortifying coffee from her cup, "may think what you want, dear lady. I can't stop you." She got up.

"Hey, wait, aren't you going to have your omelette?" Olivia asked, pointing to the gooey mess in the bowl.

"I'm not brave enough to face two challenges this morning. You eat it," Bridgette said cheerfully. She turned again to leave, thinking she could get something to eat on the plane. Food wasn't that important to her anyway. Constant dieting to keep her hundred and one pounds in nice proportion had left her with the feeling that food was something to eat to survive, not to enjoy. When she skipped meals, which she did often, she usually forgot quickly that she'd done so.

She stopped at the sound of footsteps behind her. "Are you going to follow me with that?" Bridgette asked, half expecting Olivia to be holding the bowl of raw eggs.

But Olivia's hands were free. "No. I'm getting ready to go with you," she told Bridgette matter of factly. "I didn't realize we were leaving so soon. You've got to give a girl some notice." She pushed past Bridgette to her own bedroom.

Bridgette stopped in the doorway and leaned against the frame. "The reason I didn't give you any notice is because *we* are not going anywhere."

Olivia closed her closet door and turned to face Bridgette. "But you said—"

"I said *I* was going. *You're* staying."

"But I always go with you," Olivia protested. "You know how cranky you get when you have to do everything for yourself."

"I'll manage," Bridgette told her. "Studio cutbacks," she added over her shoulder as she headed for her own room.

Olivia followed her. "Saving on one measly plane ticket? When they're spending millions to make the movie?" She sounded dubious.

"Save pennies to make dollars," Bridgette said flippantly, placing two heavy suitcases next to the door.

"You're not going to win any more awards if you talk like Ben Franklin," Olivia said dryly, pushing her aside and moving each suitcase to the large bed, then opening them.

"And just what do you think you're doing?" Bridgette demanded.

"Checking your packing. You know you always forget something when you pack." Olivia rifled deftly through first one suitcase and then the other, murmuring, "Hmm."

Bridgette watched her patiently, shifting from one foot to the other.

"Just as I thought," Olivia said, going to the lingerie drawer. Bridgette looked on as the older woman extracted a filmy light-blue nightgown. "You forgot this," Olivia pronounced, tossing aside a sensible pair of pajamas to make room for the nightgown. "You're not going to get anywhere wearing gunnysacks."

"We're not making an X-rated movie, Olivia," Bridgette protested, taking out the nightgown and replacing the pajamas. Olivia was just as quick to put the nightgown back in the suitcase. "And even if we were, I don't need *that*," Bridgette insisted, jerking her head at the nightgown.

"With your tongue, you need all the help you can get, lady," Olivia countered. "Don't think I don't know why you don't want me coming along with you. You're afraid I'll wear you down for Adam." Olivia scrutinized her. "You know, I could do a lot worse things for you."

"Yes, you could kill me with your cooking," Bridgette said, "but that doesn't mean I'll let you get away with it." She took out the nightgown and tossed it aside. "I don't need a spy working against me."

Undaunted, Olivia refolded the nightgown and replaced it. "You need fourteen guardian angels working over you just to keep you from doing something stupid again." Bridgette reached for the nightgown once more, but Olivia took a mild swat at her hand. "Now you listen to me, boss lady," she said, her voice lower and more serious. "Somebody up there is giving you another chance at what you blew before. Don't mess it up this time. Adam is the best thing that ever happened to you."

"A lot you know." Bridgette sniffed, but inside a little voice agreed. Yes, Olivia was right. Despite everything that had happened since, that one small island of time in the beginning had been wonderful, worth all the subsequent unhappiness. But she'd be damned if she would give in now. Everything had changed since that idyllic time. Adam was surrounded by beautiful women now. What did he need her for?

Bridgette licked dry lips. "Are we going to fight over my suitcase all morning so that I miss my flight?" she asked, her hands on her hips.

"That depends on whether you're going to throw out the nightgown again," Olivia told her, her fingers hovering protectively over the item.

Bridgette shrugged. "Let it stay. Just because it's there doesn't mean I'm going to wear it."

Olivia smiled knowingly but said nothing. "You want

me to drive you to the airport, or am I getting too close
to the scene if I take you there?" she asked sarcastically.

"You know, Olivia, you'd better hang onto me. I don't
think anyone else is going to put up with you," Bridgette
told her. Her tone was affectionate. "Oh, all right." She
sighed. "Don't look so dejected. You can come. I'll get
you a ticket." Bridgette shook her head. "I guess you
need a break from all the housework you tell me you've
been doing." Besides, she thought as Olivia left happily
to pack, if she kept Olivia at her side, she wouldn't be
left open to Adam's advances—if he made any, which
she doubted.

The flight to Salt Lake City International Airport was
short, but Bridgette's nervousness mounted as they drew
closer to the end of the trip. Would Adam be there to
meet her? she wondered, then banished the thought. She
was acting like a high school girl waiting for the class
hunk to call her. This was Adam. Adam the Beautiful,
she had once dubbed him. Adam, who had an adoring
following.

The thought brought a pang to Bridgette's heart as
she relived the moment of walking in on Adam and that
woman. It was as if it had happened at breakfast, rather
than over eleven months ago. That was what had kept
her up all night, picturing Adam with that . . . that woman.
Adam loving someone else. Damn him! Bridgette
squeezed the armrests hard.

"What's the matter?" Olivia asked. "This isn't your
first flight." She paused. "You really that worried about
being around him?" she asked sympathetically.

Bridgette looked up in surprise. It wasn't like Olivia
to be sensitive to her moods. For a moment she thought

of telling the older woman about the hell she was going through.

She was going back to face Adam in the midst of the kind of situation that had fanned the flames of her insecurities many times before. The girls in the movie were beautiful, all of them, and she...she was just plain Bridgette Santaniello, the ugly-duckling daughter of a former beauty contest winner and the younger, insignificant sister of the much touted and highly acclaimed Donna. Bridgette was her mother's crowning disappointment. How could she merit anything other than pity from Adam?

But her thoughts lay stillborn on her tongue, and she merely shrugged in response to Olivia's question. "I just don't like being around the desert and heat," she said, but she saw at once that Olivia didn't believe her.

A few minutes later the FASTEN YOUR SEAT BELTS sign flashed brightly before them and Bridgette concentrated on the plane's descent into the Salt Lake City airport. Olivia chattered on as if to divert her. Bridgette smiled. Olivia might not make a very good housekeeper, but she was a sterling companion.

Adam wasn't waiting for her when they deplaned.

Well, why should he be? Bridgette asked herself. He didn't know her flight number. Of course he could have made it his business to find out....

But she didn't want him here, she reminded herself, carrying her luggage past the security guards, who checked her tags routinely. The bright Utah sun gleamed down on her, and she squinted, looking for a cab that hadn't yet been attacked by a gaggle of overloaded travelers.

She hailed one and sank into the back seat with a weary sigh. "Hotel Utah, please," Olivia instructed the driver, and the cab pulled quickly away.

The driver spoke pleasantly to them. He had five daughters, the oldest of whom was about Bridgette's age and expecting her first child. The family was thrilled.

First child. The words floated through Bridgette's mind before she could stop them. She could have had a first child by now. Maybe even a second. A boy with eyes that twinkled hypnotically like Adam's. . . . If Adam wasn't such a bum, she thought, rousing herself as the driver pulled up in front of the hotel.

"This is it," he said, helping Bridgette out. Olivia followed.

Bridgette glanced up at the ten-story building, which was constructed of white brick in an ornate French Renaissance style. The outside was beautifully decorated with scrollwork and carvings of figures.

"That's quite a building," she murmured, impressed.

"We're proud of it," the driver said with civic pride as he took her bags out of the trunk and went inside.

"Oh, that's all right," Bridgette said, "I can handle those." She handed him the fare and a generous tip.

"I like doing things for people," he told her brightly, his broad face lighting up with a cherubic smile. "Makes the day go by faster."

Bridgette smiled, too, and thanked him, then turned to the desk clerk, who looked as if he had been freshly starched along with his clothes. "I'm Bridgette Santaniello," she said. "I believe you have a room for me. My companion, Olivia Thornton, will be staying with me as well."

"Oh yes," the desk clerk murmured, perusing the large register before him. "That was the overnight stay."

"Overnight?" she echoed, puzzled. She had been told

in no uncertain terms that the trip was to last at least several weeks. Had Davidson changed his mind about making her stay, after all? What was going on?

"Yes," the man replied pleasantly, "I believe the gentleman making the arrangements said something about you staying in a trailer on location after tonight." He shook his head. "I really think our rooms are far preferable to a trailer in the desert."

"I'm sure they are," Bridgette agreed. "Please reserve my room for a week," she added as a bellboy appeared to take their bags. Olivia shot her a disapproving look.

"I'm afraid I've already reserved your room for someone else after tonight," the desk clerk explained. "There's a convention in town. But," he added, pausing dramatically, "I'm sure I can arrange for another room."

"Please do," she said crisply. Trailer indeed! Adam knew she hated being outdoors. Was he trying to make her life totally miserable? She and Olivia followed the bellboy into the elevator.

The young man opened the door to the room and laid their luggage on low stands, but Bridgette hardly noticed. Was Adam doing this on purpose? He knew she loathed being away from the city. The idea of going out each day to the desert was bad enough, but staying there overnight, with the sand, heat, and whatever little creatures God had placed there was too much to bear.

"Where's the phone?" she asked the bellboy, fishing in her purse for a tip.

The young man pointed politely to the phone on the dresser, happily pocketed his tip, and disappeared.

"Well, at least the beds are comfortable," Olivia said, testing one. She looked up with a gleam in her eye. "Adam visiting you here tonight?"

"No," Bridgette said firmly. She whirled on her four-inch heels, intent on telling Harry she was going to take the next flight home if she received the slightest argument about spending her nights in the hotel. Abruptly, she stopped dead in her tracks.

The reason for her sudden halt was roses—two dozen plump, deep-red roses arranged magnificently in a lovely pale-blue vase. They were reflected in the bureau's mirror, making it seem as if there was an army of flowers clustered there. Their perfume engulfed Bridgette. He'd remembered, she thought, glancing at the card that was tucked inside. He had given her a rose on their first date, and she had told him that she loved roses. During all their years together there had been many bouquets, even before they could afford them.

Bridgette reached out and tenderly touched one rose, taking it out gently and brushing it wistfully along her cheek. She had missed the roses. . . . She had missed Adam.

She heard a soft knock on the door. Bridgette glanced up, her heart beginning to pound, and her eyes met Olivia's surprised glance. It was him. Don't do anything foolish, her mind warned her, but her feet were already moving toward the door, and paying little heed to the inner admonition.

She opened the door, her head raised high, expecting to see Adam's tall frame. Her eyes dropped slightly, as well as her spirits, when she beheld a slender man, dressed in dark slacks and a dark-blue pullover.

"Hello, Ralph," she said almost dully.

Ralph sighed. "Funny, most women sound like that when they see me in their doorway." He glanced into the room. "Okay to come in?" he asked hesitantly.

"Sure," she said with a shrug, gesturing him inside.

"Hi, Olivia," Ralph said, nodding at the other woman as he entered. Olivia humphed acknowledgment and went about giving the room a once-over. "Adam sent her roses," she said tersely. "Proves he still cares, doesn't it?" she demanded of Ralph, her eyes on Bridgette.

He grinned. "Does in my book," he said, also turning to Bridgette.

She struggled with embarrassment, annoyance, and a warm feeling for what these two friends were trying to do. "Look, you two," she said, "the Adam Reeves I knew and loved existed a long time ago. The new one doesn't need or want me, except to work on this picture and perhaps to avenge his wounded pride." She noticed a blank look on Ralph's face. "I am, after all, the only woman who ever walked out on him," she pointed out. Even if I didn't want to, she added silently. "That must have hurt his growing ego. Now let's forget the hearts and flowers, okay?" She didn't wait for an answer. "What's this nonsense about staying in the desert?" she asked Ralph, her voice assuming a slight edge.

Ralph held up thin, protesting hands. "Hey, you'll have to talk to Adam about that. It's his show. I'm just the production manager."

"Okay, production manager," Bridgette said patiently, "what are you doing here?"

"Seeing an old friend, I thought."

Bridgette's anger softened. "I'm sorry," she said. "It's just that this whole thing has me on edge. I . . ." She paused, then changed tacks. "How have you been?" she asked.

"Not bad," Ralph said, a little more relaxed. "I haven't given up completely trying to direct, but Adam thought this was a better place for me for the time being. Keeps food in my mouth and pretty girls in front of my eyes. I mean . . . um, Adam's been really good to me. He hasn't gone Hollywood or anything. Remembers all his old friends. You'll meet a few of them today on the set. Kind of like old home week."

"Old home day," Bridgette corrected tersely.

"What?" He looked at her, confused.

"I'm not staying," Bridgette told him. "At least not in some trailer that's liable to have the cooling system break down in the middle of a heat wave. I never liked roughing it, remember?"

"Path of true love never runs smoothly," Olivia interjected, throwing dark looks at Bridgette.

"You can go home on another flight, you know," Bridgette reminded her, eyeing her archly.

"You see what I have to put up with?" Olivia asked Ralph.

Bridgette turned to him. "Good help is hard to find these days."

"So are good bosses," Olivia muttered.

Bridgette gave up. She turned to Ralph. "Besides saying hello, are you here under orders?"

"I've come to drive you to the location. It's in the Great Salt Lake Desert."

Bridgette closed her eyes momentarily and sighed. "Might as well give it the once-over—once," she said, resigned. "Let's go."

"Um, aren't you going to change?" Ralph asked, eyeing her lavender skirt, and deep-purple blouse, and matching high-heeled shoes.

"No, why should I?" Bridgette wanted to know, expecting only to be given a quick tour of the set.

Ralph merely shrugged and muttered, "The car's downstairs."

"Good place for a car." Bridgette led the way out of the room.

She tossed the rose she had been holding to Olivia, who caught it and yelped. "It's got thorns!"

"Doesn't everything?" Bridgette asked with another resigned sigh. "See you later."

The trip to the film crew's location took over an hour and was bearable only because of the car's air conditioning. Bridgette hated heat. She had spent twenty some odd years in New York, hating the sticky, oppressively humid summers. California had been a godsend for her with it's mild temperatures. What was she doing traveling into a desert, she asked herself, subjecting herself to heat and Adam, two things in life she most wanted to avoid? She glanced at Ralph.

"So, how have you been doing?" she asked good-naturedly.

"Good, good," he replied, nodding.

"Found anyone yet?" she asked, genuinely interested.

"Nope—but looking is great!" He grinned broadly.

"I suppose being with Adam gives you a wide variety to choose from." She stared straight ahead, hoping she didn't sound as interested in the answer as she really was. Her common sense damned her for having said anything at all.

Ralph guided the car expertly over some bumpy terrain. They were off the main road now, and the ground rose and fell without warning.

"Not really," he said. "Adam's mostly involved in his work."

"Oh, come on, Ralph. I can read. I've seen the gossip

columns. He's out with a different girl every night. He seems to be setting up his own private harem."

Ralph shrugged helplessly. "He was trying to forget you."

"Uh-huh," Bridgette said, utterly unconvinced.

"Oh, there was a girl a while ago," Ralph answered. "Pamela. I thought it was pretty serious." Bridgette felt a tight knot growing in her stomach. "She was a real lady and—*hey!*" he cried sharply.

Ralph swerved the car to avoid hitting a camel, which seemed to have loped out of nowhere. They came to a full stop as the animal undulated by, followed soon afterward by a harried looking trainer.

"I take it we're here," Bridgette said as she dropped her hand from the dashboard, where she'd braced herself. She wanted Ralph to finish his story, but he was Adam's best friend, and she knew that he'd immediately report any spark of interest on her part back to Adam. She wasn't about to give him the satisfaction of knowing she was curious about his love life.

"Yes, we're here," Ralph told her, getting out.

"I guess I have to get out of the car." Bridgette sighed, eyeing the disappearing camel warily. It looked as if the production was having problems already.

Ralph laughed as he opened the door for her. "I'm afraid so, Bridge," he said, giving her a free hand.

She took it as she got out and immediately sank down in the sand. Four-inch heels were apparently not the ideal footwear for sandy terrain. She caught Ralph looking at her shoes as he held her up, but he didn't say anything. Ralph knew better.

"Where's the Great Director?" she asked with false brightness.

Ralph shrugged, looking anxiously about the wide, flat terrain. From his expression Bridgette surmised that he hoped to be rid of her soon.

She shaded her eyes from the glaring sun and looked around. As far as the eye could see, brilliant, almost unearthly white sand simmered back at her. To the far left several trailers were strung in single file, looking out of place in what could easily be mistaken for the area once known as Palestine—the Holy Land of over a thousand years ago. The place was just what the movie called for. To the extreme right stood a grove of magnificent looking horses, kept a safe distance from the camels, whose particular odor, Bridgette knew, could panic the relatively untrained horses. Immediately before her gaily striped tents had been set up. She saw one or two actors dressed in appropriate costumes milling about in front of the larger tent.

Still shading her eyes, she looked at the horizon and saw what appeared to be a tall, bronzed god riding toward her, his wheat-colored hair haloed magnificently against the brilliant blue sky. His clothes accentuated his powerful, sensuous body. He could have been the leading man in this picture, Bridgette caught herself thinking as Adam rode up.

Suddenly a wave of heat rose up inside her that had little to do with the soaring temperature. For a brief moment she thought she was going to faint. And then her eyes locked with Adam's. . . .

5

BRIDGETTE FELT AS if he had touched her, despite the distance still separating them.

What foolish, romantic thoughts kept popping into her head, she thought. Yet she couldn't take her eyes away from his compelling figure. He was mounted on a beautiful white stallion that looked as if it had come straight out of Valentino's *The Sheik*. Indeed, that was the image she was trying to create in her screenplay when the heroine first set eyes upon the knight who was to be her savior.

The assistant animal trainer, who was now holding a camel's reins tightly in one hand, walked by Bridgette.

The animal's hooves sent up a cloud of dust that blew straight into her eyes. She blinked several times, trying to clear them. When she opened her eyes again, a scantily dressed blonde was standing directly in Adam's way. As her eyes cleared further, Bridgette saw that it was Sindee Allen.

Bridgette watched spellbound as Adam brought his horse to a halt.

He bent his head to listen to something Sindee was saying, but didn't dismount, as if to indicate that he had other pressing business. From where she stood, Bridgette could see Sindee pouting prettily, gesturing in exaggerated motions at her costume and whirling about, as if doing a dance.

"She planning on doing a seductive fertility rite out here in broad daylight?" Bridgette asked Ralph dryly.

He offered her a weak smile in response and shrugged his thin shoulders, looking in Adam's direction. "Sindee's been complaining ever since we got here this morning," he told Bridgette. "She's turning into a royal pain."

"Looking like that, she'll be forgiven I'm sure," Bridgette said coolly, noticing the way the gauzelike skirts swirled about the woman's well-proportioned hips.

Ralph said something else, but Bridgette didn't hear him. She realized that Adam was riding in her direction. Despite the warnings flashing in her mind, despite the glaring inadequacies she felt when looking at Sindee, Bridgette couldn't stop the rushing of sensation that came over her as Adam drew near.

"Welcome to Shangri-La," he said warmly, gesturing grandly.

"The pits is more like it," Bridgette said darkly as he dismounted next to her, brushing against her body as he did so. A flash of electricity darted through her and she stepped back, almost falling as one heel sank deeper into the sand.

Adam's strong hand darted out to catch and steady her. The touch of his fingers on her arm made her feel weak inside. C'mon, girl, you're made of stronger stuff than that, she admonished herself. You can lick this.

Adam's gleaming smile indicated his amusement, which irritated Bridgette. "You keep tugging like that and you're going to wind up sinking into the sand up to your neck." He glanced down at her legs as she pulled one heel out of the sand. "You should be wearing boots, or at least flat shoes," he told her. "Didn't Ralph tell you he was bringing you out here?" He looked toward the production manager, who shrugged.

"Yes, he told me, but I don't own a pair of flat shoes," Bridgette said with exasperation, "and I have no intention of becoming a desert creature."

"Practicality was never your long suit, was it?" Adam said, his easy grin a flash of white on his rugged, tan face. The dimple in his cheek deepened.

"If we're going to discuss faults, let me get out my list of yours," Bridgette said archly.

Adam held up his hands. "Truce, truce. I surrender for now in the interest of getting this picture going."

Bridgette shrugged. "Okay, I'm not unreasonable."

She didn't like the amused look that came into Adam's eye at her words, but he turned to Ralph without commenting. "Get the costume designer here right away. Tell her to bring her sketch pad, her patience, and a couple of seamstresses."

"What's up?" Ralph asked, fishing the car keys out of his pocket.

"The prima donna doesn't like the way her dress flows. She thinks she's overdressed for the harem scene." Adam smiled.

Indeed, if anything, Bridgette would have judged that Sindee was underdressed for everything but a centerfold. "Why don't you just offer her a large gauze bandage?" she suggested. "She can trim it down to size."

Adam laughed, then said, "Get on with it, will you, Ralph? I'll see you later to give you tomorrow's shooting schedule."

Ralph grinned and saluted. "Right," he said, looking relieved as he slid back into the driver's seat. "Oh, the video equipment is supposed to arrive by two o'clock."

"Good." Adam nodded.

"Hey, wait a minute," Bridgette cried as Ralph started the motor. "What about me?" Her voice was almost a wail. She didn't want to stay in the hot, broiling sun. She could almost feel beads of perspiration forming at the back of her neck.

Adam slipped an arm around her shoulders. "I'll take care of you," he said, his voice husky. He waved away a grateful-looking Ralph.

Bridgette stiffened, trying to steel herself against the effect of Adam's touch. "I can take care of myself, thank you," she said firmly. She nodded toward Sindee, who smiled seductively at Adam, then disappeared behind a tent flap. "Who picked Sindee for the role of Princess Joanna? I okayed Sondra Sullivan."

After having pictured her heroine as a delicately regal young woman, Bridgette was irritated at having the role taken over by a brassy, fluffy blond.

"Sondra had another commitment," Adam explained.

"And Sindee's your latest flame, I take it," Bridgette couldn't help saying. She felt the old jealousy creeping over her, making her act totally unlike herself, making her hate the words that seemed to spring to her lips of their own accord. It wasn't supposed to be this way. She was supposed to act cool. Cool? In this weather? The weather was partly to blame, she told herself. The rest of the blame belonged to Adam.

"Sindee is Davidson's niece," Adam told her.

Bridgette nodded. "How convenient for you," she heard herself say.

Adam stopped in his tracks and turned her to him with a hard hand on her shoulder.

"Don't you ever stop?" he demanded.

"Don't you?" she countered, alluding to the women in his life. She stopped herself. "Look, this isn't going to get us anywhere," she said, struggling to be her normal, rational self.

"Oh, I don't know," Adam said, his voice softening as a light came into his eyes. "After our earlier arguments, we used to wind up in bed," he reminded her.

"Speaking of which," she said swiftly, brushing aside the obvious, "why is my reservation at the hotel for only one night?"

"Because I need you close to the shooting. A lot in the script doesn't quite work," he told her, his tone now businesslike.

"Now don't start that again!" she snapped. "There might be a couple of lines here and there—"

"More like a couple of dozen scenes here and there," Adam corrected firmly.

"Now you listen to me, Adam Reeves"—Bridgette

tried to rise on her toes to be closer to his eye level and almost threw herself off balance—"I don't know how big your head's gotten in the past eleven months, but I'm not a hack writer. I might not be good at much, but I'm good at writing. If you recall, that's what paid the bills while you were going to school."

"No argument," Adam told her. "But some things don't work visually, even though they make very good reading." Then a smile came to his lips. "And you're wrong, you know."

"Oh?" she asked archly, expecting more of an argument from him.

"You're good at more than writing," he said with a wink. "I can remember you being very, very good when the lights were low." His voice drifted over her body like a warm, seductive hand.

"That was a long time ago," she said firmly, drawing herself up to her full height. She tottered dangerously on her heels, but refused the hand he held out.

"Perhaps," he told her softly.

"There's no *perhaps* about it," she said firmly, determined not to give in to his temptations. She wouldn't let him break her heart again.

He ran a finger slowly along her chin. "Too bad. Okay, then go to work, Ms. Santaniello," he said crisply, acting like a director. "First order of business is that you take off those damned shoes. Or I'll carry you around, if you'd prefer," he offered, his eyes twinkling.

She slid the shoes off her feet, grabbing them up by their straps, almost yelping at the hot sand on her nylon-covered feet. She was decidedly shorter without her shoes on too, and didn't like having to stare up into people's

faces as she trudged after Adam, who took long strides
ahead of her.

He turned around, cocking his head. "I'll get you a
spare pair of flats, but until then let's keep up, shall we,
Ms. Santaniello? Everyone pulls his weight around here,
or they get replaced."

"Barbarian!" she muttered.

"Don't flaunt your Romanism at me, Santaniello" he
said, laughing. "You Romans only stole from the Greeks."

Bridgette clenched her teeth as she followed him,
determined not to leave herself open to any more barbs.

"Is it all settled, Adam?" Sindee purred, emerging
suddenly out of the tent as Adam approached. She took
possessive hold of his arm.

Bridgette pretended not to notice. It was none of her
concern now, she told herself as she gazed out at the
sprawling terrain, shifting from foot to foot and watching
the people working quickly to set up their equipment and
living quarters. Others were busy building sets out of
huge jigsawlike pieces that must have been shipped from
the movie studio. A miniature town seemed to be coming
to life.

"Ladies and gentlemen," Bridgette heard Adam call
out, and she turned to look at him. Apparently Sindee
hadn't managed to pull him away to her lair. Bridgette
smiled as Adam climbed on the roof of a hard-topped
jeep to address the people on the set.

A crowd began to assemble. Camera operators, grips,
best boys, stunt people, actors and actresses had soon
gathered around him. Adam waited until everyone could
hear before continuing.

"As you well know," he said, grinning engagingly,

"I believe in having a lot of rehearsals and doing very little shooting until the scenes are just the way we want them. We're all professionals here, so we shouldn't have much trouble getting this project launched. If we all do our jobs, we can be out of this heat in two or three weeks, back to our snug little beds and our nice, cool sound stages. So, let's get to work, shall we?"

The group shouted in agreement and clapped enthusiastically. Bridgette marveled at Adam's ability to take command. He was always in firm control but never tyrannical. His mere presence seemed to establish a mood of camaraderie on the set, while fans and professionals alike respected his great talent as a director. Bridgette had even heard that several of the crew members had taken cuts in pay to work with him.

She watched proudly now as Adam climbed down from the jeep and began shaking hands warmly with members of the crew, shouting greetings and slapping people on the back. But her lips tightened when he kissed a buxom brunette wearing tight jeans and a tall redhead in a clingy pullover. Same old Adam, indeed!

One man, a lanky fellow in his late thirties with sandy hair and a mustache, fell in step with Adam. They approached Bridgette, who was still standing with her shoes slung over her shoulder.

"Bridgette, I'd like you to meet Rex Billings, our cinematographer," Adam said. "Rex, this is Ms. Santaniello, our writer." From Adam's tone, Bridgette could tell he would like to have said more, but for some reason he didn't.

Rex extended a bony hand and shook hers. His fingers were remarkably cool considering how warm it was.

Bridgette's clothes were already beginning to stick to her body.

"I've admired your work for a long time, Ms. Santaniello," Rex said, and Bridgette couldn't tell if he was sincere or just being kind.

"Thank you."

"Rex has found just the right location for the battle scene between King Richard and Saladin," Adam told her. "I thought you might like to see it." His deep jewel-green eyes stared down into her upturned face.

She roused herself from their mesmerizing effect. "No, I think I'll just stay here and—"

But her words were cut off as Adam propelled her toward two horses. Rex followed.

Bridgette glanced at the big white animal Adam indicated to her. "I don't ride, Adam," she reminded him, hoping that would be the end of it.

"You know how to sit, don't you?"

"Yes, but—" Adam picked her up and threw her into the saddle. She was momentarily thankful that her skirt was wide enough for her to sit astride. Then his high-handedness made her forget everything. She began sputtering with indignation—and was further surprised when Adam mounted easily behind her.

"That's all you have to do, just sit. I'll do the driving," he told her, flashing a smile. "Lead on, Rex." He waved the man on.

Bridgette didn't like sitting so close to Adam. Her flesh tingled despite her resolve. His strong arms encircled her protectively and pulled her even closer as he held the reins. Her back pressed against his warm, broad chest.

"Comfortable?" he asked in a low voice that tickled the back of her neck.

"No."

"Good." He chuckled.

"You're insufferable!"

"No," he murmured softly into her hair, making all sorts of funny things happen inside her, "just impatient. Very impatient." The next moment he called out to Rex, "How much farther is it? I think our unwilling traveler is getting cranky."

Bridgette hated him for making fun of her. Usually she got on very well with people. If she seemed irritable, it was only because of the heat—and him. Well, she'd just have to try harder. She didn't want anyone to suspect what being with Adam was doing to her. No doubt people were already gossiping about Adam Reeves and the woman he had divorced.

"Don't exaggerate, Adam," she said in a pleasant tone that caught him off guard. She sensed him looking down at her in surprise. "I'm very interested in seeing the site Rex has found," she added brightly.

Rex turned and smiled. "It's just a little farther," he promised, waving his hand in the general direction.

Bridgette knew that it was up to the cinematographer to set up the composition and movement of a scene, following the general instructions of the director, who usually developed his ideas from key words in the script. This time, they were in total harmony, for the area that Rex had scouted out looked exactly the way Bridgette had envisioned it.

She glanced back to see Adam's reaction. He nodded slowly, his eyes sweeping over the terrain. Bridgette could almost see the thoughts forming in his mind, so deep was his concentration. And then his mood broke.

"Perfect!" he told Rex. "We'll do this scene first. Have them set up the cameras for—"

"Scene forty-two," Bridgette interjected.

Adam smiled down at her. "Scene forty-two," he echoed, nodding. "You're still sharp-witted as well as sharp-tongued, I see."

Without answering, Bridgette turned to Rex. "It *is* perfect," she said. "Just what I imagined when I wrote it. With King Richard's men charging in from the west, beating back Saladin's Saracens until the turning point in the battle . . ." She glanced up at Adam. "You *will* let Saladin's men win, won't you? Or do you intend to have me rewrite history to suit your purposes?" she asked sweetly.

"We'll discuss that later," he told her, kicking the horse's flanks and riding about the area, guiding the horse in a wide circle. Rex and his mount waited off to the side.

"You're making me dizzy," Bridgette complained. "What's Rex going to think, watching you ride around like you're on some merry-go-round?" She knew he was doing this just to tease her. She didn't like the desert, didn't enjoy being on top of a horse, and definitely didn't want to be this close to Adam. He was purposefully prolonging their stay.

"Rex will think I'm taking in the atmosphere," he replied. "And I am," he added, his mouth so close to her neck that she could feel the warmth of his breath. "The sights out here are very lovely today."

"Very pretty words, but they're wasted on me," she said, trying to keep a lump from forming in her throat.

"Too bad," Adam said as he turned the horse around

suddenly and rode back to Rex. "Okay, I think we've seen enough. We can use the area to the far right for the camp scene," he said as Rex pulled a small pad from his breast pocket and scribbled down a few words.

"I thought we could set up the castle walls of Acre over there, toward the west," Rex pointed. "The scene in which Richard's sister is abducted by the Saracens."

Adam considered the matter, then nodded his approval. "Just as the sun is setting," he suggested. He looked down at Bridgette. "What do you think?"

She was surprised he'd asked for her opinion. As she studied the area that Rex had pointed to, she tried to imagine a stone castle silhouetted against the sky. The sun sinking behind the walls would cast just the right light as the infidels stormed the castle in search of the woman who had captured Saladin's fancy. She nodded her agreement. "I think you're on to something," she told Adam.

"I hope so," he said softly.

The ride back wasn't fast enough for Bridgette, yet it was over all too soon. She had to hold on to her defenses, she told herself. Otherwise, she'd be lost. Adam had always been her downfall, her one weakness. Now he was so much more dynamic and forceful than he'd been when she'd first fallen in love with him—and twice as hard to resist. He was even better looking, if that was possible. She had a hard fight ahead of her, but she mustn't give in, or further heartache was sure to follow.

He didn't need her anymore. He was extremely successful, and he had his pick of gorgeous women. What they had once shared was gone, and there was no point in torturing herself with memories. He was cruel to tease her like this, she decided, raising her anger like a protective shield. Yet the pain of loneliness and betrayal cut through her anger and left her yearning. . . .

She breathed a sigh of relief when they reentered camp. Adam dismounted behind her. She slid off after him.

"You did that better than I thought you would," he said.

"I've learned to do a lot of things in eleven months that might surprise you," she said and walked stiffly away.

6

BRIDGETTE RETURNED TO the Hotel Utah at seven fifteen bone tired and eager for a hot shower. She should have been back hours ago, she thought, annoyed. Better yet, she shouldn't have gone in the first place. They hadn't really needed her. She'd pointed that out to Adam when she'd gotten hold of him again, which hadn't been easy. As soon as they'd returned to camp, he'd been surrounded by members of the cast and crew, all asking questions, all demanding his time. Finally, when she had gotten his attention, Adam had flashed her a disarming smile and told her he wanted her to get the general feel of the set. He promised he'd talk to her later about the changes he wanted in the script. But between setting up the equipment and outlining the rehearsals, which he wanted to get underway immediately, he hadn't found time to say three words to her.

When Bridgette had tried to locate a car to take her out of the blazing desert sun and back to the hotel, she hadn't found one available. She'd had to wait several hours before a crew member was able to give her a lift.

Right now, she felt dusty, tired, and upset over the prospect of spending the next few weeks in those torture-chamber conditions. It might be even longer if they didn't stay on schedule. And these days few movies did. Adam had earned the reputation of bringing in his pictures both ahead of schedule and under budget, which was probably why Davidson had snatched him up. But she heard that Adam had just finished making another picture and hadn't even had a week to rest and make notes for this project. Suddenly, she wondered why he'd agreed to take a new project so soon. He'd often told her he didn't want to burn himself out.

Well, that was his problem. She would stay only for a week. If he didn't like it, that was also his problem. After her shower she would call Harry and tell him so in no uncertain terms.

But first, the shower. Bridgette could almost feel the water cascading soothingly over her body, the hot water beating away her tension and fatigue.

She passed the front desk and trudged toward the elevator. Her stockinged feet rubbed grittily against her high-heeled sandals. Oh, she was going to hate every minute she was out here, she just knew it—and so did Adam, the beast. He was keeping her here just to be spiteful. Well, she'd show him.

"Olivia?" she called out, entering her room.

But her companion was nowhere to be seen. A note on bright-pink paper, Olivia's favorite shade, caught Bridgette's attention. She kicked off her shoes, silently blessing the man who had invented air conditioning, and read that Ralph had come by and offered to take Olivia out to dinner. Never one to turn down a free meal, Olivia had accepted.

Bridgette thought it was odd that Ralph had taken Olivia out instead of having come back to the set to drive her home. Oh well. She was in no mood to listen to Olivia extolling Adam's virtues anyway.

As if to haunt her, Adam's face suddenly popped into her mind, blotting out everything else. The image refused to be banished as she stripped out of her perspiration-soaked clothing and got into the shower. As the steam rose, coating the silvery wallpaper with beads of moisture, his face grew more and more vivid, sending tingles through her wet, steaming body.

Why was she doing this to herself, she demanded fiercely. Adam didn't care about her anymore. She was just a pawn to tease and tantalize. If he'd cared, he wouldn't have let the divorce become final.

She finally forced herself to step out of the shower, away from the cocooning heat. She toweled her body hard, rubbing away the languid feeling that had stolen over her.

She was just tired, she told herself. And whose fault was that? Adam's. He was getting even. Well, they would see who'd win this round, she promised, slipping into a silky blue robe and combing her short, wheat-colored hair.

She reached for the phone and ordered a sandwich

and a diet soda from room service, then dialed Harry's number.

He wasn't happy to hear from her, she could tell. "Give it a little more time," he urged.

"I'm going to give it as little time as I can, Harry," she said firmly. "You know how irritable I get in hot weather. And there's absolutely no reason for me to be out here, roasting in a tin box."

"A tin box?"

"A trailer," she clarified.

He chuckled. "Bridgette, studio trailers are hardly tin boxes. Some of them have more of the comforts of home than home."

"I'll roast," she repeated.

"Bridgette, I just want what's best for you. Think of your career, all those years we put in together getting your work seen by major movers and shakers." His voice took on a nostalgic tone, and Bridgette sighed. There was no reasoning with Harry, when he turned wistful. "Besides, Adam's the best and he's—"

"Harry, please," she interrupted, sitting down on the bed, defeated. "Don't talk to me as if I were a three-year-old child. And don't," she warned, "tell me Adam's the best thing that ever happened to me. I'll hang up on you if you do."

"No," Harry said, "I'm the best thing that ever happened to you. Adam's the *next* best thing."

Bridgette laughed and felt a little more like her old self. "Okay, Harry, I'll stick with it for a little while. But there's no reason for me to stay the full time."

"Find a reason," he urged.

She bid good-bye to Harry. He was afraid of what Davidson might do if she left the set, but she could handle

Davidson. She could handle almost everyone, except Adam.

During their marriage she had never "handled" him, but she had supported him with her enthusiasm and her faith. He had needed her then, and she had never felt so alive, so fulfilled. But once he had tasted success, and things had begun happening so fast that they were both left breathless, the dream had ended. He hadn't needed her anymore. He had secretaries typing letters for him and a manager planning for him, and she'd been left on the outside, swept aside as the crowd cheered him on, taking him farther and farther away from her. Adam had been too caught up to even realize what had happened.

Sadness gripped her. She stepped out onto the balcony to watch the sky grow dark above her eighth-story window. It had finally grown cooler. Oh, it was all too complex to sort out. She'd feel better once she ate, she reasoned.

As if on cue, someone knocked on her door.

"Who is it?" Bridgette asked, tying her sash tighter.

"Room service," came the muffled reply.

"Thank goodness!" she cried, crossing the room and throwing open the door. The first thing she saw was a table with two place settings and a covered platter that was much too large to conceal just a sandwich.

The second thing she saw was Adam.

"That's the kind of greeting I like," he said, pushing the table into the room, followed by a bellboy. Bridgette stood to one side, flabbergasted.

"What do you think you're doing here?" she cried.

"That's the kind of greeting I was expecting," he said with good humor. His eyes swept over her, seeming to look past the material of her robe to the naked body underneath. Bridgette felt exceedingly uncomfortable.

"To answer your question, I'm bringing your dinner," Adam said, rolling the table next to the balcony.

"This isn't my dinner," Bridgette informed him. "My dinner is a cheese sandwich."

"The hotel mouse ate all the cheese, so they hoped you would accept this as a substitute," he said, uncovering the center platter with a flourish to display a rack of lamb bouquetiere. "This is from the Roof Restaurant," he told her, referring to the famous restaurant on the premises. "It's their specialty."

"Why two plates?" she asked suspiciously.

"Lonely eating by yourself," he said, placing the platter cover on a nearby table. "Remember, our movie deals with romance. We have to keep you in the proper mood if you're going to make the right changes."

"Our movie?" she repeated. She had only thought of it as *her* movie. But it *was* his as much as anyone's, she realized. After all this time they were sharing something again, and a small, secret part of her was glad.

Adam looked down at her as she stood on the lush brown carpet. *"Our* movie," he repeated, his voice caressing her.

She was about to say something when Adam produced a bottle of champagne from a paper bag.

"You have to drink," Adam said in response to the dubious look Bridgette gave the bottle.

"I have to go to bed," she told him, and immediately realized her mistake when a mischievous look came into Adam's eyes.

"All in good time, Bridgette, all in good time," he said, grinning.

The bellboy coughed to mask a smile. Bridgette grabbed her purse and pulled out several bills she came to. "You can go now," she said haughtily.

Adam stayed her hand. "Women's lib be damned. Put it on my bill," he instructed the bellboy. "I ordered it, I'll pay for it." He tipped the boy.

"You can bet you'll pay for it," Bridgette said meaningfully.

The bellboy nodded, muttered "Good luck" to Adam, and was gone.

"Well, you certainly gave him something to think about," Bridgette said coolly.

"And what about you? Have I given you something to think about?" he asked, coming up behind her and gliding his hands ever so lightly up and down her arms, making waves of hot shivers dance through her body.

She turned, clenching her fists beneath the long, wide sleeves of her soft blue robe, fighting the feelings his touch awakened in her, feelings he alone had the power to evoke. "Adam, I appreciate your ordering dinner for me, but—"

"Then let's eat," he said, pulling out a chair. As he pushed it under her, her robe parted and fell away from her legs, exposing firm, trim thighs. Bridgette moved to close it, but to her surprise Adam tucked it neatly back into place for her. But not before his strong fingers brushed against her flesh, making her ache. A pulsating sensation beat rhythmically through her. He was playing with her!

But his expression was all innocence as he seated himself opposite her, smiling beguilingly.

"You know," he said, picking up an embroidered white napkin and spreading it carefully on his lap, "there was a time when we could only look at pictures of food like this and daydream about when it would be our turn to live like kings."

"Well, the daydreams have all come true," Bridgette said with a touch of asperity.

"Ah yes, but at what a price," he said, regarding her significantly.

"Please don't start," she warned.

"It never ended," he replied, his voice deep and low.

"Everything ended." She turned her attention to the salad. *Please,* she thought, *please don't touch me.* A little voice, barely noticeable, countered with a wistful *"Please do."*

But Adam just studied her for a moment, silently, making her feel terribly ill at ease.

"Adam," she said finally, "why do I have to stay on the set?"

"I told you, we need to make changes."

That tack had gotten her nowhere before, and she resented his tampering with her story, which she had researched carefully and struggled for long hours to write. She knew it was her best work, and she felt protective toward it.

"If you recall," she said, "I'm a city girl. That means my body has to be near a city at least three hours a day or I break out in hives."

"I recall everything about you," Adam said in a voice that Bridgette thought would have melted a weaker woman right then and there. It silenced her for a moment, and Adam looked pleased at the effect he was having on her. He was insufferable!

"I don't care for the great outdoors," she persisted. "Unlike you, I do not thrive on being surrounded by hundreds of barren acres and coyotes."

"You certainly write about it with a flourish and tenderness," he said, baiting her. "Why, in *Frontier Paradise* you—"

"What I write about is one thing," she interrupted. "What I feel is quite another. I'm a professional. I don't have to feel everything I put down. That's what imagination is all about."

"Oh yes, your imagination," Adam said knowingly, and she felt annoyance rising within her, in response to his highhanded manner. He made her feel like such a fool. "Well, I hate to tell you this," he continued, "but your imagination seems to have deserted you when it came to the romantic dialogue. It's stilted."

Her brows shot up as she watched him savor a mouthful of lamb. He looked like a small boy. He hadn't lost his appreciation of life. Each morning, she remembered, he'd jumped out of bed as if the day had been made just for him and he didn't want to waste a minute of it.

Bridgette brought herself up short. What was she doing, making a testimonial to him? The man was attacking her work!

"I've never written anything stilted in my life!" she said indignantly, her cheeks growing warm with anger.

"Well, then I guess someone snuck in and erased all your lines, because what I read . . ." He shook his head. "You've done better, Bridge. You've done a lot better. I guess you've been away from the scene for too long," he added, and his smile challenged her. "I could remedy that."

She took a deep breath. "If you're inferring that I have no romance in my life, you're flat wrong! As a matter of fact, romance is one of the reasons I want to get back to L.A. I had to leave someone behind—someone special I don't want to be separated from," she concluded in a rush.

To her disappointment, Adam looked only mildly interested. His expression seemed to prove once and for all that any feelings he might have had for her had long since died.

"Who is he?" Adam asked disinterestedly.

"That's my affair," she replied coolly, happy for once with her choice of words.

"Well, the poor devil obviously isn't getting your best if this is all you can come up with," Adam said, referring to the script. Bridgette felt her temper getting the best of her, and she stabbed her fork into a piece of lamb. "I think it's dead already," Adam said dryly, watching her. He rose.

"What are you doing?" she asked suspiciously.

"Getting up to pour the champagne. Don't be so skittish."

"I'm not skittish, I just don't trust you. You play dirty."

"I play to win," he said, smiling.

"I know," she answered, meeting his eyes as he handed her a fluted champagne glass filled to the brim. "How many women have you added to your collection since I saw you last?" she asked sweetly.

"Don't ask stupid questions, Bridge," he said, suddenly angry. "Your imagination is still working overtime."

She sighed and took a sip of champagne. She hadn't eaten much food, and she felt the effects of the champagne almost immediately. "Look, let's be honest with each other," she said, finding it suddenly easier to say what she was really thinking. "On a scale of one to ten,

I'm a four." She gestured to herself, then slung out a hand toward him. "And you're a ten and a half."

He threw back his head and laughed. "I promise I won't enter the same beauty contest you do."

"That's right, laugh," she said, annoyed as she drained her glass, which Adam immediately refilled.

"I always laughed when you babbled, remember?" he said. "And you're not a four, you're an . . . eight."

"You see!" she shot back.

"Bridge," he said patiently, "if I said you were a ten, you'd call me a liar." He moved his chair closer to hers. "Can we compromise at nine?"

She shook her head and drank several more gulps of champagne. "That wasn't the point I was trying to make."

"No, that's not the point at all. The point is I didn't marry you because you were some stupid number on a scale, but because you were you—and they haven't invented a number that could capture the essence of you. They never will." He whispered the last words, making her shiver as he filled her glass once more. "Without that damned defensive wall around you, you're something very special."

"You're trying to get me confused," Bridgette muttered. Her senses were already reeling, half from the champagne and half from the feelings he was arousing in her.

"I'm only telling the truth," he said softly.

"Finish your lamb," she ordered, pointing her knife at his plate.

He moved his chair back in place, seemingly satisfied with her response. "Yes, mother," he said with a twinkle in his eye. He glanced around the room. "Nice accommodations."

"Yes, too bad I won't be using them," she said, suddenly remembering that he had banished her to the desert. The desert. In July. How could he? "Look, couldn't I just stay here and messenger the work to you?" she suggested. He had been so nice a moment ago. Maybe this was the time to strike.

But he shook his blond head from side to side. "Nope. I might need you for an instant rewrite."

"What do you think I am? A slot machine? You put in a quarter and get a new script?"

"You were fast, as I recall."

"Fast, yes," she agreed. "Incredible, no."

"Oh, I thought you were pretty incredible," he said. She didn't know quite how to take that, so she left it alone. "I see you got my roses," he said after a bit.

She turned to them. "Oh, yes. That was very nice of you. You always were thoughtful when you wanted to be." Which was why sending her out into the desert was that much harder to endure. He was up to something, she was sure of it.

"I'm a very thoughtful person, didn't you know? Speaking of which . . ." he said, reaching underneath the table. Bridgette watched, not knowing what to expect next. "This is for you," he said, pulling out a huge package.

She stared at the box. "It's not ticking. It won't explode," he assured her. "Take it."

Vexed by his laughing tone she almost snatched it away from him.

"Opening it usually tells you what's inside," he said watching her.

Bridgette rose and placed the box on the bed, then opened it quickly, uncovering high laced boots, several pairs of designer jeans, and five T-shirts in different colors. She turned to look at Adam and found him right behind her.

"All your size," he assured her.

"Why?"

"After seeing you sink into the sand this morning, I didn't want to take a chance on losing you before the picture was over—at least not until you've completed your rewrites. I knew you hadn't packed anything practical. You've never been very sensible."

Bridgette chose not to rise to the bait. To her surprise, Adam put his arm around her shoulders.

"And think of all the fun you've missed in the past eleven months not being able to save me from my own folly," she said. "Why did you ever give me up?" She tried to keep her voice light, despite her racing heart, hoping he'd accept her question as teasing banter.

But his voice was soft and serious when he answered, "I was tired of the accusations, Bridgette. I was tired of always being on the defensive."

"Welcome to the club," she said, thinking of her present situation, then adding, "So what are you doing here?" She struggled against the effects of his nearness.

His eyes were steady on her as he drew her against him, his hand brushing her breasts as he pulled her close. His breath caressed and warmed her neck, sending hot tremors all through her body. He pressed her intimately against him, making her fully aware of his hard length.

"I keep remembering the good times," he whispered. "I've missed you, Bridgette." He turned her around to face him, his eyes shining with a special light that used to be for her alone. "I've missed the smell of your perfume, the funny way you have of tilting your head when you're thinking. I've missed the feel of your body curled up against mine."

She was sinking fast. "Um, Olivia will be back any minute," she said, attempting halfheartedly to escape his grasp.

"Don't count on it," he told her, a smile curving his lips. "Ralph eats slowly." He kissed the hollow of her throat.

Bridgette's lips tightened with suspicion. "How did you know . . . You arranged it!" she accused, the light dawning suddenly.

"You talk too much," he told her, and slowly, inexorably, his mouth came down on hers.

Further accusations died on her lips as she became lost in his kiss.

7

ADAM KISSED HER, his lips lingering for precious moments, his hands tracing a warm path down her back and
around her waist. His touch brought to vivid life memories of what it had once been like between them, when
they'd been together without accusations, without hurt
feelings, with nothing more than love on their minds.

Bridgette trembled with anticipation and cursed herself for even thinking of making love with him. She
refused to be one of his many women! But her body
ached for Adam as he cupped her face in his hands and
lifted her mouth to his once again. He teased the corners
of her mouth, his tongue stroking her full lips until Bridgette thought she would scream with wanting.

She fought hard not to touch him, to will herself to

think of other things, to recall the pain of finding him with another woman. But nothing worked. She was helpless in his arms, desperate to express the love she still felt for him.

His mouth covered hers, working its magic, drawing her soul away as he kissed her more and more passionately, making her head swim, her pulse race, and her body yearn for his familiar touch.

Adam's sure fingers progressed languidly along her throat to the opening of her robe. He gave a gentle tug to the lightly tied sash and the robe parted seductively, exposing her firm, high breasts. He brushed them lightly, then slipped his arms possessively around her, his hands burning her flesh.

She felt herself being lifted onto the bed. There was no escape. He was kissing her, burning her, making voices within her cry out to him. It had been almost a year since they'd been together. An eternity.

She reached up and brought his head down to her. He buried his face in her neck, his tongue a gentle rasp along her skin. She moaned and twisted, savoring the feel of his hands and mouth, and craving more.

The sound of Adam murmuring her name heightened her excitement and enveloped her in a vast wave of pleasure. Her doubts and painful memories fled. Nothing mattered but having him in her arms.... Later she would remember and repent her weakness, but now was for loving.

Somehow, without leaving her side, Adam managed to pull himself free of his clothing. His strong, virile body was like a hot imprint against hers as her passion soared. They seemed to be propelled into a timeless space as they clung together.

Adam cupped her breasts in his palms and brushed his thumbs lightly over the sensitive nipples until they stood full and proud. He kissed one lovingly, then the other. "Wouldn't want it to feel deprived," he whispered, smiling down at her, his voice husky.

And then his expression became utterly serious, full of an emotion she had once thought was love. "Bridgette, my Bridgette," he murmured. "Welcome back."

She had no chance to wonder what he meant as his hands moved over her with a new urgency. He caressed her breasts, shoulders, back, hips, and buttocks. He held her tightly, molding her to his hard body, stroking away her remaining uncertainties and stoking her inner fires to fever pitch.

Now her impatience matched his own. They sought each other restlessly, and came together with an intensity of feeling that tore a cry of pleasure from her throat. Adam surged inside her and she met his thrusts with eager abandon, her head thrown back and her body arched. She felt poised on a peak of glorious pleasure that claimed and held her enthralled, then sent her falling, falling all limp and languid in Adam's arms. Joy swept over her like a powerful wave as she lay breathless and panting, her fingers smoothing locks of hair from his damp forehead. She ran her hands lightly, slowly, over his back, unable to keep from touching him.

But as she lay there and Adam, too, touched her and kissed her cooling skin, doubts intruded to disturb her sense of peace. Now that the heat of passion had passed, she felt weak and vulnerable before him. She had given in too easily. She'd let him destroy her defenses with almost no resistance. She had betrayed herself.

No matter how much she wanted to, they could never

go back to the way things had been before. Her feelings for him hadn't changed and never would, but his feelings for her had changed irrevocably. She was only one of many women in his world now. What lasting attraction could she possibly hold for him?

Angry tears clouded her vision. Why, oh why, had she allowed herself to be so weak? He'd been playing a game with her, getting even, and she'd handed him the victory without a fight.

Bridgette forced herself to get out of bed. She was afraid to look at Adam, afraid she would see triumph in his eyes.

"What's wrong?" he asked mildly, turning to watch her.

"Nothing's wrong," she said, digging deep inside for a masking bravado. "I just wanted to prove something to you."

"What?" His voice had suddenly acquired a hard edge.

Bridgette kept a confident smile on her lips. "Really, Adam, do I have to spell it out?" When he said nothing, she added, "Did my response just now seem like that of a woman who had been away from romance for too long?" she asked, pulling her robe around her.

Adam studied her for a long moment, then shook his head slowly, the light seeming to slip away from his eyes. "No," he said, rising. "It certainly wasn't." He shrugged carelessly. "Maybe you *have* been practicing."

His words cut her to the quick. They held no trace of jealousy. He didn't seem to care.

Of course he didn't care, she told herself. That was what she'd been trying to tell herself all along.

"I haven't been practicing nearly as much as you," she couldn't help saying. "For a while I thought you took a photographer along on every date."

"Not *every* date," he said with a grin that looked almost cruel.

"Oh, I forgot," Bridgette said, hiding her pain. "Ralph said you're serious about someone." She fought to sound disinterested as she knotted her sash with a firm tug, but her heart was pounding.

He looked mildly surprised as he pulled his shirt over his broad muscular chest and buttoned it swiftly. Bridgette could hardly keep her eyes off him. He pulled on his jeans with jerky motions, gliding the worn material over trim hips. Bridgette checked an impulse to reach out and touch him.

"Oh, you mean Pamela," he said casually, but something about his tense stance, clenched jaw, and cold gaze made her wonder if he was hiding a very deep anger.

"Yes, Pamela," she repeated in a hollow tone.

He shrugged. "Pamela was a bright, thoughtful, considerate girl I went out with a few months after you and I broke up."

"She sounds divine," Bridgette replied, trying not to care. So, he *had* found someone else.

"She was everything a man could want, I suppose," he added heading toward the door.

"So what happened?" She had to force the words past dry lips.

He looked back at her, his eyes suddenly soft. "She wasn't you," he said quietly, then closed the door behind him.

Several sleepless hours later Bridgette heard the door open softly. In the light cast from the hallway she saw Olivia tiptoe in. "You can get off your toes, Olivia,"

Bridgette said. "He isn't here." She sat up in bed.

Olivia snapped on a light, blinding Bridgette momentarily. "Why not?" she asked, her hands on her hips.

"Because," Bridgette said, squinting against the glare, "he got what he came for and left." She looked away, ashamed of the way she had phrased that.

Olivia came around the bed to look at her. "That doesn't sound like him."

"That," Bridgette said with a sigh, "is what I've been trying to tell you all along. He's changed."

"Oh?" Olivia said loftily as she placed her purse on the nightstand. "Then why did he arrange to be on this picture?" she challenged.

"What?" Bridgette stared at Olivia, suddenly wide awake as she took in this new piece of information.

"That's right," Olivia said smugly. "I got Ralph to spill the beans. Albee's not sick," she said. "Adam got him to fake it. Albee's got a little ham in him, it seems."

But Bridgette hardly heard the last sentence. "Faked it?" she echoed. Then Adam *wanted* to be on this picture—*her* picture.

"That's what the man said."

"But why?" she said aloud, hugging her knees to her chest.

"Because, you ninny," Olivia said, sitting down on the bed next to her, "despite your jealousy, Adam still loves you and wants you back. Can't you see that?"

"Olivia." Bridgette sighed and shook her head. "You see what you want to see." She smiled sadly. "Good old Olivia, always in there pitching. He's not interested in me anymore. He stopped being interested the first time the studio set him up for publicity pictures and put him on the arm of that voluptuous starlet."

"Then what's he doing here?" Olivia demanded.

"He wants to get even."

"Even!"

"I walked out on him. I wounded his ego. He can't handle that. He wants to prove that he can still have me whenever he wants to, and he wants to give me a hard time in the only sphere I still have left to me—my work." Bridgette didn't want to believe what she was saying, but she couldn't logically see any other explanation, especially after what had happened that night.

Olivia waved away her words. "You're getting paranoid and melodramatic," she pronounced, rising.

"No." Bridgette lay down again and turned her face to the open glass door leading to the balcony. She stared into the inky blackness beyond the filmy curtains, but all she saw was Adam's expression when she'd implied that she'd had other lovers.

Ralph came to pick her up the next morning. Olivia had decided to stay in town and do some shopping. Bridgette dreaded seeing Adam again. Now that he knew she was an easy mark, it would be even more difficult to keep her distance. Now that the memory of being held in his arms was so fresh, it would be impossible to resist his touch. But she must. They must deal together on her terms, not his. She loved him, yes, and would take him back in an instant if he really wanted her, if he really loved her. But he didn't want her, and he certainly didn't love her. It was a game to get even, nothing more.

She and Ralph were silent on the way to the set. "A penny for your thoughts," he said finally.

Bridgette turned to him and sighed. "Your penny's worth more than that, even with inflation."

"Oh, I don't know. We used to be pretty good friends before separate camps were established. If you recall, I was *your* friend before I was Adam's."

"That's right," she said, suddenly animated. "Why did you take his side?"

"I identify with the underdog," Ralph said in all seriousness.

"Underdog! You men just stick together," Bridgette accused lightly.

"Have it your way, Bridgette, but someday you'll find I was right." Ralph's tone was patient.

"And I suppose I imagined all those women throwing themselves at Adam."

Ralph shook his head. "No, they're real. Lord, are they real," he muttered longingly. "But you can't blame a guy for wanting to enjoy all that attention just a bit, can you, Bridgette? After all, it is a bit heady. But Adam's got things in perspective now," Ralph added quickly, casting a sidelong glance at her.

"Sure, sure," Bridgette said, nodding dismissingly. They let the subject drop.

It was barely seven o'clock when they arrived on the set, but various activities were already underway. "Where's Adam?" Bridgette asked.

"Probably in his trailer," Ralph said, smiling broadly as he pointed it out.

"Your face is going to break, Ralph, if you keep smiling so hard. I only want to get the discussion of my rewrite over with," she said nonchalantly.

"Sure, sure," he said, echoing her previous comment as he headed in the opposite direction.

Bridgette approached the long trailer that was first in the lineup. To the right, where a tent had been set up as a canteen two sleepy-eyed attendants were setting out breakfast for the crew. Bridgette hurried over, got two styrofoam cups full of black coffee and walked into Adam's trailer without knocking.

He was bent over a large notebook with mounted pictures, the movie's story board. He looked up, surprised.

"Don't you knock?" he asked, accepting the coffee. "Or are you hoping to catch me again?"

"So you finally admit to that hanky-panky!" she exclaimed. She hadn't thought he'd ever own up to the truth.

"I'm admitting to the fact that you caught Rhonda trying to seduce me, that's all," Adam explained.

"Uh-huh. You still take your coffee black?" she asked, changing the subject.

"You still shy away from the truth?" he asked. "Why are you so bent on convicting me?" He studied her over the rim of the coffee cup as he took a long sip.

"The judge believed me," Bridgette retorted, coming around to look at the drawings on the story board.

"The judge was a senile old man who wanted to get the case over with so he could take his eleven A.M. nap. He would have granted a divorce to Romeo and Juliet!"

"If Juliet had the goods on Romeo . . ." Bridgette let her voice trail off meaningfully.

Adam threw up his hands. "You haven't changed, Bridgette. Part of me is glad—and part of me wants to strangle you!"

"You do, and the Screen Writers' Guild will be on your neck," she teased him, smiling in spite of herself.

"I'd rather have *you* around my neck," he said, his voice softening. "Like last night."

"Last night," she said, tensing, "was a mistake."

"Yes," he agreed. "It should have happened sooner. A lot sooner."

"You said you had some script revisions for me to work on," she said, changing the subject once again.

Adam sighed. "All right, Bridgette, we'll play it your way for now, but don't think you can get away with this forever. Yes, I've made notes of the script revisions I'd like you to make." He dug beneath a sheaf of papers, upsetting the story board.

Bridgette reached out for the large bound notebook. "You still do your own story board?" she asked, flipping over the drawings, each of which depicted an individual scene in the movie.

"A perfectionist, that's me," he said with a smile.

"You still can't draw worth a damn, you know." She glanced at the sketches.

Adam took the book from her. "Well, this isn't Walt Disney Studios, so I should be forgiven."

"You know, the cinematographer could probably do a much better job," Bridgette told him, thinking what would be most professional.

"I'm sure his pictures would be neater, but he doesn't see the project the way I do. Besides, he's got enough to do," Adam said, waving his hand.

"And you don't?" she countered.

He grinned. "I like you mothering me."

"I'm not your mother," she said sternly.

His grin grew wider. "I'll say you're not," he agreed.

"Forget last night," she insisted.

"Not in a million years," he said, his tone both teasing and wistful.

She drew herself up to her full height, wary of another

assault in her vulnerable being. "That's about how long the memory will have to last you," she countered.

Before she could move out of his reach, he leaned forward and ran his finger along her lips, his eyes twinkling merrily. "I don't think so."

She pulled back. "The pages, please."

"Okay, here." He dumped a pile of notes, both long and short, into her hands.

"There're more pages here than pages in the script!" she protested, staring at the mass of papers.

"You're exaggerating again."

He sounded as if he were talking to a little child, which provoked her, as did his all-knowing manner. "Maybe you'd like to rewrite the script yourself!"

Adam glanced at her. "I don't have time. Besides, that's what they're paying you for, isn't it? Now stop being so protective of your work and read my notes. I need the first three scenes by this afternoon."

"This afternoon! In case you haven't noticed, your job doesn't come with a whip!"

"Quiet, or I'll chain you to your trailer and feed you only bread and water." He winked.

"That's about your speed," she muttered, glancing through the notes as she headed out the door—and almost collided with Sindee. The actress was wearing her costume from the middle of the picture, which, on her, looked like spun tissue paper. Bridgette resented the fact that her fair and gentle heroine had been turned into a vamp.

"Sorry," Sindee said, paying little attention to Bridgette. Her brown eyes were on Adam. "Just look at this," she wailed, spreading out the nearly transparent skirt.

"I am, I am," Adam said with an appreciative laugh

that made Bridgette's back stiffen and her heart sink.

"I look like an old washer woman," Sindee protested. "Just look," she cried, thrusting out her full breasts, which Bridgette considered very scantily covered indeed. "She's covering me up! How can I look sensuous in the harem scene?" she demanded, swirling seductively around Adam, her hips speaking a language all their own.

"You're an actress, aren't you?" Bridgette said sweetly. "Act. It might be a new experience for you."

With that parting line Bridgette fully intended to make her exit, but this time Ralph barred the way out. He looked slightly disconcerted and was perspiring more than the heat warranted.

"We've got a problem, Adam," he said.

"I'll say we've got a problem," Sindee pouted, turning to Ralph. "Just look at this!" She spun around in a swirl of floating fabric. Ralph's throat worked dryly. Adam looked as if he had had just about enough.

"Sindee, I'll talk to the costume designer later," he promised. "Now be a good girl and learn your lines, okay?"

Sindee left, casting a smug look at Bridgette, who was now more concerned with what Ralph had to say.

"Okay, Ralph, what's up? The camels staging a strike?" Adam asked.

Ralph shook his head. "Davidson sent a studio man to oversee the production," he reported gloomily.

From Ralph's tone, it didn't sound as if the studio had sent the typical, genial sort of man who merely kept to the shadows, enjoying the prospect of getting paid for rubbing elbows with movie stars.

"So?" Adam asked.

Bridgette could tell that he didn't like the idea of being

watched. No one else had seen fit to impose such a restraint on him, and for Adam it indicated a vote of no-confidence. The man's presence would cast an uncomfortable pall about the set.

"You have to see this one. He's wearing a bow tie," Ralph said as if that explained everything.

Adam sighed. "Let's go and be nice," he said with resignation. He stuck his story board under his arm and followed Ralph out. Bridgette fell in behind him.

But as they emerged from the trailer, Adam turned around and said, "The changes, Bridgette. I need those changes."

"Not before I get to see this obstacle course," she said, and for the moment they were on the same side of the team.

Adam flashed her a grin and put his arm around her shoulders as they walked behind Ralph. "You look good in that," he said, glancing at her T-shirt and jeans.

"I look like a poster for an Army recruit," she corrected, recalling Sindee's sensuous costume.

"Have it your way," Adam said, shrugging.

Before them stood Davidson's handpicked overseer, a man who for all appearances had never smiled in his life. Despite the growing heat he was dressed in a gray, three-piece suit with a descriptionless shirt wilting beneath the jacket and an old-fashioned bow tie.

"Never trust anyone wearing a bow tie," Adam said to Bridgette between lips that barely moved.

She tried to hide her smile as she looked at the portly, florid-faced man who stood mopping his brow, sliding an elegant handkerchief over his thinning hair. His body was shaped like a pear, with small shoulders and a wide bottom. He appeared displeased at having to be here, enduring the heat and dust. Clearly the man spelled trouble.

"Harold Beamish," he said, extending an unusually white limp hand toward Adam.

Adam took the hand and gave it his accustomed hearty shake. The other man's hand moved as if it was disjointed, and Adam let it drop. "Adam Reeves," he said. "This is Bridgette Santaniello, our writer."

Small, piggish eyes regarded Bridgette for a moment before dismissing her. Beamish turned back to Adam. "Mr. Davidson told me about her," he said in a voice that spoke volumes and provoked her anger. No doubt he'd been informed that her last script had caused the studio to just break even. She was going to be under scrutiny, as well.

"I take it Ralph has shown you around," Adam said pleasantly.

"I never let an underling fill me in, Mr. Reeves," the man said through pursed lips. Bridgette and Ralph exchanged glances. "I promise I do not mean to waste your time. I do not mean to have any time wasted whatsoever," he said pointedly, staring at the crew, who were, for the most part, merely standing around watching. Several members either shifted their gazes or moved elsewhere. "But I do wish that you would be the one to take me on a tour, as it were, of this godforsaken area."

Adam nodded. "Very well."

Bridgette knew he was annoyed at having his plans upset. He had scheduled rehearsals to take place first thing that morning, and he liked to keep to his schedules. Adam glanced around for his assistant director.

"Aaron," he called, "start Owens and Marshall on

Scene 95," he said. "Run through it a couple of times. I'll be back presently." The young man nodded and immediately set to work.

"Is that a sign of your authority?" Beamish asked, his round face turned toward the departing Aaron.

"That's a sign of respect," Adam said pleasantly. "Now shall we get on with it?" he suggested, glancing at his silver-faced watch. "My time is rather limited."

"I've made it my business to run on a schedule," Beamish said grandly. "It's nice to meet a man in this business who has a healthy respect for the studio's dollar."

Bridgette watched the two men disappear and shook her head. More and more it looked like this was going to be a long production. She could foresee nothing but problems with Beamish. And what did he mean to her professionally? If they ran behind schedule on this picture, she might begin to get a reputation as studio poison. It wasn't difficult in these times of tight money to frighten off would-be investors. Bridgette tried to push the thought out of her mind as she headed toward her trailer.

Bridgette stopped where she was when she spotted Joel Sommers, the young waiter Adam had talked to at the Brown Derby. So, she thought, Adam's instincts had been right after all. The man had obviously passed his screen test.

"Hi," Bridgette said brightly, coming up behind Joel. "Remember me?"

Startled, the young actor spun around on his heel, and the sword dangling at his side almost took a swipe at Bridgette's leg. She jumped back, and a few of Adam's notes floated out of her grasp onto the ground—where they probably belonged, she thought cynically.

"Oh, gee, I'm sorry," Joel apologized. He swooped down to pick up her papers and his sword rose dangerously toward her again.

Bridgette laughed. "I think I should stand ten paces away until you tame that thing," she said, pointing to the upturned sword.

Joel looked up at her sheepishly, then offered her the gathered papers. "I'm sorry. It's all so new to me," he confessed.

"And exciting, I bet," Bridgette said, remembering how she had felt when she'd been the new kid on the block.

He nodded vigorously. "I feel like a star-struck kid."

"Good," she said. "Don't lose that." She looked back at Beamish's roly-poly figure as he struggled to keep up with Adam's long strides. Bridgette grinned. She recognized Adam's trick of walking that way when he wanted to annoy someone. He'd used it often enough on her! "We're going to need a lot of your enthusiasm before this picture's over with," she told Joel, then went back to her trailer to work.

8

IT WAS A nice trailer as far as trailers went, but although it might have had all the comforts of home, it still wasn't home. Bridgette felt as if she'd been in it forever. She sat staring down at the scribbled corrections and suggestions that Adam had demanded she take into consideration. A pile of newly typed pages was stacked neatly to one side.

"Tyrant," she mumbled, putting another sheet of paper into her worn IBM Selectric, which she had brought with her. Although she could use other typewriters in a pinch, she claimed she did her best work on "old faithful."

A knock sounded on the door, and Bridgette glanced

up. "Come in," she called, erasing the line she had just written.

Adam's large frame filled the room.

"Come to see how the prisoner is doing?" she asked sarcastically.

He grinned and picked up the pages next to the machine. "Very well, it appears," he said.

"Never let it be said that I'm not cooperative."

"Now who'd ever say a thing like that?" he asked innocently.

She glanced up at him, then back at her typewriter. "Don't get cute," she warned.

"But you're the one who said I couldn't help that."

"How was Beamish?" she asked ignoring his comment.

"Interesting," Adam said, after some thought. He leaned against her desk to peruse the pages. "Very interesting. He could be a big problem for us," he told her, reading what she'd written.

"Maybe he'll go back after a few days out here."

"Not likely," Adam replied, shaking his head.

"I can't understand why anyone would want to stay here if he didn't have to," she said seriously.

"He has to," Adam said, still reading. "He's Davidson's most trusted man, and Davidson is panicked that we'll fall behind schedule."

"And will we?" she asked, looking at him intently.

"Not if I can help it."

"But with the changes you want—" she began.

"Then get them to me faster," he told her, making her angry. So if they fell behind schedule, he'd blame her. Was he out to discredit her?

Why was he doing this to her? Was he so intent on

getting even with her for rejecting him that he'd purposely cast her in bad light with Davidson and ruin her career? Oh, what had happened to the Adam she used to know? Why had he changed so much?

He continued to study the changes she'd made. "You didn't rewrite the second speech," he said suddenly.

She stood on tiptoe, looking over his shoulder, and glanced down at the speech in question. "It doesn't need to be rewritten," she declared firmly.

"It doesn't work the way you have it."

"Try it out," she insisted.

"Change it."

"I won't change it until I see them try it out." She glared at him, her hands on her hips. "That's my final word on the subject!"

Adam shook his head. "Bridgette, you never have a final word. There's always a word after that and a word after that..." His voice trailed off.

"Is the right to give out verbal abuse one of your fringe benefits as director?" she wanted to know.

He nodded. "It's written into my contract. Right after the clause about getting all the free women I want." He eyed her wickedly.

"You're hopeless!"

"And you're still as sharp-tongued as ever." She opened her mouth to say more, but he stopped her by placing a finger on her lips. His voice was soft. "You weren't the easiest woman in the world to live with, Bridgette. But the only thing harder than living *with* you is trying to live *without* you. What do you say we give it another try?"

Those were the words she had longed to hear him say, but how could she believe them, especially after his threat to blame her if they fell behind schedule? He must be trying to get her off her guard so she wouldn't realize what he was actually doing. He was planning to discredit her. Well, she was no one's fool now, not even his.

"No," she said crisply.

Now he looked surprised. He shook his head. "You know, for a flowery writer you certainly could have drawn that out a little more," he told her casually, and his manner seemed to indicate that, just as she'd suspected, he didn't really care.

"You're only trying to get me to agree with your changes," she accused him. "Now take the scene the way it is and get out of here. Sindee is undoubtedly waiting for you, dressed in a Band-Aid and complaining that it's too large." She shoved the pages back into his hands.

"So now you're going to be jealous of *her,* are you?" He sounded amused.

Anger shot through her. "Sometimes you get me so mad, I—"

He didn't let her finish the sentence. Instead, he pulled her against him and his lips covered her unwilling mouth in a forceful, demanding kiss. Bridgette tried to keep her lips closed against the onslaught of his mouth, but she found she could no more resist him than she could stop the passing of the seasons. Her lips parted, and she felt the teasing touch of his tongue inside her mouth, causing electrical currents of excitement to ripple through her. A tingling sensation grew in her breasts.

With considerable effort, she managed to squeeze her hands between their bodies and push him back. "You're not going to win that way either," she said, trying not to sound as breathless as she was.

"Fun trying, though," he returned lightly.

"Let me go."

"As you wish." His hands fell away from her almost instantly. "Can I at least direct you to the lunch wagon?" he asked, his eyes twinkling.

She acquiesced to that. "I'm not unreasonable."

"Ha!" was all he said as he held open the trailer door as she stepped outside. They walked over to the canteen tent and stood at the end of a long line.

"You kissed back, you know," he whispered into her hair.

"I was being kind," she lied.

"You were being terrific," he told her. She glanced quickly up at him and flushed when he winked.

Lunch was far from exciting. The broccoli had been overcooked into a puree, and the roast beef was ten degrees past well-done. The sandwiches looked a bit dried out, but they appealed to Bridgette more than the other selections. She chose a ham and cheese on rye, and picked out an apple. She liked her apples cold and this one was decidedly warm, but it would have to do. She fished a can of diet soda out of a pool of water then wove her way toward a table.

Adam was right behind her and slid in next to her, crowding her. She was acutely aware his warm thigh was brushing hers, but when she shot him a warning look, he only smiled. The devil, he knew exactly what he was doing to her. She glanced down at his tray and saw that among other items, he had a jar of imported sausages, his one weakness since he had "made it."

"Where did you get these?" she asked.

"Private stock," he told her. She might have known. "Want some?"

She shook her head. "I hate them."

"How can you say that?" he asked, trying to spear one out of the tight jar.

"Watch my lips," she said, pointing. "I hate them," she repeated slowly, and then took a bite out of her sandwich.

"I like watching your lips," he said.

"Quiet," she chided, not wanting to be a source of gossip on the set.

"Ever wonder how they get these little sausages in here?" Adam asked, examining the jar.

"I think they stand them up and build the jar around them," she said dryly, taking a sip from her soda can.

"Very clever," he remarked. "See if you can put some of that wit into your script."

"I already did," she replied coolly, "but only a full-wit can see it. It's above half-wits." With that, she rose, fully intending to take herself and her tray elsewhere.

"You haven't finished your meal yet," Adam said, gripping her wrist tightly and stopping her dead in her tracks. "You've got to keep your strength up if you intend to be creative. If that was a sample, you need second helpings." His words mocked her, but his voice was firm.

Bridgette's anger rose another notch, and she was about to reply when a voice said, "Mind if I join you?" She turned to see Joel carrying a tray loaded with at least one of everything available.

Adam waved Joel closer and indicated a seat next to Bridgette. "When did you last eat?" he asked, looking at the tray, from which several items seemed in imminent danger of falling.

"This morning," Joel answered, sliding next to Bridgette, who sat down again also. She felt trapped but decided to make the best of it. After all, she liked Joel.

Adam laughed. "Well, at least there's one person who appreciates this food. Eat heartily, Joel. I want to watch you do that scene we talked about yesterday. Just as soon as that has a chance to settle to the bottom of your stomach," he added, pointing his fork at the leathery looking wedge of roast beef on Joel's plate.

Joel nodded vigorously. "Mr. Reeves, I just can't tell you how grateful I am. I hope I won't be a disappointment to you. I—"

"You'll be fine," Adam said in a firm, soothing voice that indicated his confidence in the younger man.

Watching, Bridgette marveled at how masterful Adam had become. From the almost shy, quiet man who had needed her to bolster his shaky self-confidence, he'd become an effective leader, a man who was sure of his own strength. He'd come a long way since they'd first met. He didn't need her at all. No, things could never be the way they had been in the old days, she thought with a pang of regret. She was a fool to even consider the idea.

After lunch, Adam began rehearsals. Not wanting to go back to work just yet, Bridgette decided to watch. The crew assembled about four miles east of the main camp at the location Rex and Adam had chosen for a confrontation between the hero and his page. The cameramen used filters to simulate a night scene.

It should be a simple scene to shoot, but Joel was an untried actor who might require special handling. Adam believed in rehearsing over and over again until the actors got the scene just right. Then he would call for the cameras to film it, and they'd complete the scene in one or two takes rather than wasting countless feet of film. It was an approach that Bridgette knew the studio heads approved of, especially since ECO stock, which was the film they used for outdoor shots, was very expensive.

In this scene the leading actor had sent his page to try to arrange an audience with Princess Joanna. Joel, as the page, had discovered that she'd been abducted by Saracens, who were acting on Saladin's instructions. Now Joel had to break the news to his volatile master as best he could.

Nervous about doing a good job, Joel choked at every rehearsal. His voice was squeaky; his face alternated between utter panic and a total lack of expression. He became increasingly distressed each time Adam said to take it from the top. The lead actor's impatience didn't help matters, Bridgette noted, wondering if Adam had made a mistake in choosing Joel after all. Out of the corner of her eye she saw Beamish taking laborious notes and shaking his head as he wiped the perspiration from his forehead.

"Okay, Joel, once again," Adam said patiently, placing a hand on the young man's shoulders.

"I'm sorry," Joel mumbled, looking down at his feet. "I know I'm making a mess of it."

"There!" Adam shouted. "That look. That's what we want. Talk to him the way you're talking to me."

Bridgette saw a look of confidence come into Joel's eyes. The next time he did the scene, it was perfect.

"Okay, this time it'll be a take," Adam called, looking to his left and then his right. "Rex," he called to the cinematographer. "Cameras!"

Rex called his camera operators, who suddenly came to life. Best boys were positioned in front of the three cameras, ready to focus them at a moment's notice. Directly behind them stood crew members who operated the video cameras, which allowed Adam to see quickly exactly what he had filmed. Bridgette remembered that they used to have to mail the film to the studio and wait until the courier brought back the daily rushes, sometime two or three days later, depending on their location.

The next scene went better. Now that Joel had more confidence in himself, he caught on quickly. As it turned out, the next scene was also the next scene in the script, which didn't happen often. Adam turned a questioning eye toward the continuity girl, who made sure everything was exactly where it had been at the end of the preceeding scene.

"Pamela?" he asked.

Bridgette's ears perked up at the name. Was that the woman Adam had been serious about? Was she the same Pamela? And if so, what was she doing here? Was Adam still interested in her? Had he stopped just for a momentary dalliance with his ex-wife while he kept his true love interest around?

Bridgette looked the woman over carefully. Dressed in jeans and a soft pink tank top, she was beautiful, someone more in Adam's league.

Pamela nodded to indicate that everything was just as it had been when the camera had stopped rolling in the previous scene.

Ralph walked by Bridgette just then, and she grabbed his arm. "Is that her?" she asked without preamble.

"Is *who* her?"

"Pamela," she said, nodding in the direction of the young woman who was now standing next to Adam. They looked quite nice together, she thought miserably.

She was taller than Bridgette, closer to Adam's own height. She'd never get a stiff neck kissing him goodnight. "Is that *the* Pamela?" Bridgette persisted.

Ralph looked uncomfortable, and she could tell by the way he shifted from foot to foot that this was indeed *the* Pamela. Her heart sank even before he answered.

"Yes," Ralph said. "But that's over," he added quickly.

"Then what's she doing here?"

"Her job?" Ralph offered meekly.

"Please drive me back to the trailer." Bridgette turned beseeching eyes on him. She felt defeated. She'd sworn off Adam once, she told herself firmly. What did this matter now? But it did, it did.

Ralph looked toward Adam. "I guess he won't need me for a few minutes," Ralph said. Bridgette knew that Ralph's job began once filming and rehearsal stopped. It was up to him to make sure that everything was ready for Adam. This included informing all the actors of the next day's shooting schedule, logging the scenes that had been shot that day, and generally keeping all the technical aspects flowing smoothly. Some people looked down on the job of production manager as that of a glorified "gofer," but Bridgette knew that Ralph considered himself Adam's right-hand man and never resented doing what some people might consider menial tasks. Adam never placed any unreasonable demands on him, either.

"I don't want to get you into trouble," Bridgette said, glancing warily toward Beamish. "Just point out a car I can use."

"The cars are my responsibility, too," Ralph said, smiling. "Ten minutes won't matter. Let's go."

They arrived at Bridgette's trailer a few minutes later,

and she threw herself into her work. Her fingers flew over the typewriter keys as she hurried to make the rest of the changes Adam had requested. Like a true professional, she forced herself to forget Adam. For a short, peaceful while, only the land of the Third Crusade existed for her, its sands shimmering beneath the baking sun of Palestine.

During the next few days Bridgette tried to keep out of Adam's way. She took her meals at odd times, when she knew he was busy on location. She tried to lose herself in her work and to spend her spare time with people on the set.

The evenings were the hardest on her. She half expected Adam to come barging into her trailer at any moment. Half expected and half hoped.

But he never did come, and she grew more depressed and agitated. By the third night she told herself he was probably with Pamela, who, she noted, rarely left his side during filming.

Very early Friday morning Adam entered Bridgette's trailer looking like thunder. "What's this?" he demanded.

Bridgette had just begun to feel awake and, still wearing a robe and pajamas, she figured she must look like something the cat had dragged in.

"What's what?" she asked, sitting down at the littered work table. Where was Olivia when she needed her? Probably out mingling with the people on the set, something she always did when she was on location with Bridgette. Despite her acerbic comments, Bridgette was sure the older woman was just a bit star-struck.

"This!" Adam said, waving a handful of papers in

front of her face. "Ralph brought them over to me this morning. Said you gave them to him last night and that these were the changes I asked for."

"They are," she said, shrugging.

"I didn't ask for King Richard to sound like a moron," he said, slapping down the papers. "Bridgette, this stuff is awful. You wrote better than this when you were doing jingles for the advertising firm back in New York." He ran his fingers through his hair. "Bridgette, I've got a lot on my mind. The last thing I need is to have you dry up on me."

"Maybe I've got writer's block," she snapped. "It happens in tense situations."

He grabbed hold of her shoulders, his large hands seeming to swallow them up. "What's going on in that muddled head of yours now?" he demanded. She lifted her chin defiantly. "Why this cloak-and-dagger routine, sending me pages through messengers?" he continued.

She tried to pull free of his grip, but found that she couldn't. She didn't want him holding her. She didn't want him anywhere near her.

"You have enough women fawning all over you," she said. "I'm surprised you even missed me." Her voice was cold.

"What fawning?" he almost shouted.

"Sindee Allen looks like she has no bones in her body when she's around you, leaning against you, melting at your feet." She hoped that would be enough to put him off.

"Sindee Allen would melt against King Kong if she thought it would get her some place. She's not as stupid as she looks. The woman is trying to make the most of

her face and figure while they're still beautiful. Next?"
he demanded curtly.

Bridgette had no choice but to mention the real problem.

"And then there's Pamela," she said quietly.

"What about Pamela?" Adam asked, eyeing her
closely.

His tone alarmed her. He sounded protective, and she
couldn't stand it. "Why are you bothering with me?" she
said finally, her voice rising. "Pamela seems to be everything you ever wanted in a woman. You said so yourself.
And I've seen you talking together, laughing together.
You fit . . ." Unable to go on, she turned to hide her
tears.

He put his hands on her shoulders, but she shrugged
them off. "Of course, I don't blame you," she said.
"She's pretty—even beautiful. And—"

"I also said she wasn't you," Adam reminded her,
cutting in softly.

"How fortunate for her."

"I'm beginning to think so," he said mildly.

Bridgette turned to look at him. "What?"

"You've certainly got your own devil to deal with,
don't you, Bridgette?" He gripped her shoulders hard.
"Damn it, you're the only rival you ever had. I can't see
how someone as intelligent as you are—at least on paper," he added pointedly, infuriating her, "can miss a
point so obvious. You were the only one holding us back
from living happily ever after."

"It's a little hard to live happily ever after when you're
by yourself," she shot back. "You were never home, and
when you were there were always projects to read through

and the phone never stopped ringing. Nothing but breathless women on the other end of the line."

"All right," he said, sighing. "I admit I was a little swept away with the blinding light of success. There was still a lot of the Iowa farm boy in me then, and I was awed."

"You were more than that," she said crisply, looking away.

"But both of my feet are planted very firmly on the ground now. I've got my priorities straight. And I'm not going to let your lack of self-confidence ruin this picture."

"So the picture is all you care about," Bridgette accused sarcastically.

Without bothering to answer, he pulled her into his arms, the force of the action so great that her robe fell open, revealing a pair of very practical pajamas. Adam seemed not to take note as he pressed his lips to her, molding her against his body and destroying any urge to resist.

9

DRUNK. SHE FELT DRUNK. But no wine could produce the heady sensation that the taste of his lips gave her. His scent excited her, and brought back memories of a thousand and one moments of shared passion. Despite all the months since their separation, his effect on her was as powerful as ever.

Expertly, familiarly, his hands caressed her over and over, stirring a flame of desire deep inside that made her tremble with longing. His tongue danced lightly across her lips, then demanded access, filling her mouth with sweet tastes and sensuous delights.

Suddenly she realized that her robe was gone and she

was lying on the bed. Adam's skillful fingers were unbuttoning the pajama top, then burning her flesh with
urgent caresses. He cupped and massaged her breasts and
she arched against him, her nipples growing pink and
hard. She yearned for the feel of his hot mouth. Finally
he lowered his blond head and kissed her neck, finding
the sensitive place that made her soar to a higher plateau
of pleasure.

She thrust her breasts toward him as his mouth found
first one nipple and then the other. Quivering, she pressed
his head against her, wanting more, wanting time to stop
still so that there would be nothing else in the world but
the two of them—no movie, no other women, no pain.
Just love and—

A loud knock on the door intruded on her paradise.
Startled and dazed, Bridgette looked up at Adam, who
rose from the bed, a look of deep annoyance and smoldering passion in his eyes.

"To be continued," he whispered into her hair as he
buttoned her pajama top and handed her the robe. He
went over to the door.

"Adam, are you in there?" Ralph called.

Adam opened the door, and Ralph fairly bounded in.
He took one look at the two of them and mumbled an
awkward apology that was swept away in the face of his
more urgent message. "Look, I'm really sorry you two,
but I think you'd better come, Adam."

"Now what?" Adam demanded, already heading out
of the trailer.

"It's Rex and Beamish," Bridgette heard Ralph say
as the door closed.

Through the window Bridgette saw Adam stride
quickly away. She tried to slow her still racing pulse.

He had done it to her again, filled her with longing for him, then simply gone off, his mind completely occupied with the problems on the set. Maybe nothing else mattered to him. She certainly didn't. If she did why wasn't his breath as ragged as hers was now? How could he turn his feelings off so quickly?

"Because he doesn't care, dummy," she said to her reflection in the tiny bathroom mirror as she washed her face and put on her makeup. But she couldn't wash away the feel of his hot lips on hers. "Men don't have to care. They just go through the motions," she said, brushing her hair with angry strokes. But something tiny and precious within her refused to believe that. One lone candle in the cathedral of her heart burned at the altar of love and hoped against hope.

When Bridgette joined the set, Adam was still trying to settle an argument between Rex and Beamish. Apparently Beamish had gotten hold of the script from Pamela and the shooting schedule from Ralph and was now trying to tell Rex how to set up his cameras.

"It would save time and money if you didn't go running off to every sand dune to take different shots," Beamish told Adam. "Just move the cameras around a bit." He gestured a pudgy hand at Rex. "In the so-called name of art, this man is milking the studio of thousands of dollars. Time is money."

"The man talks in embroidery samplers," Bridgette stage-whispered to Olivia, who stood next to her, listening. A large group had gathered to watch the argument.

"I heard that!" Beamish said waspishly, turning to Bridgette.

Adam shot her a warning look and took hold of Beamish's elbow. "Yes, time *is* money, Mr. Beamish," he said, leading the man away but still within Bridgette's earshot. "And the longer we stand arguing, the more money we're wasting. Now consider this. We could take all the shots here, but the movie-going public isn't stupid, Mr. Beamish. They'll recognize similar places no matter how much you turn the cameras around. And the public becomes resentful if you try to hoodwink them. You don't want this picture panned, do you?" Adam smiled serenely down into Beamish's round, sweaty face.

"All right," he relented, still clearly annoyed. "You win. Carry on," he ordered with a broad wave of his hand. He moved to one side, looking decidedly uncomfortable in his dark suit and wilting bow tie. Anyone who dressed like that in the desert heat deserved to be uncomfortable, Bridgette couldn't help thinking.

"Maybe we should get him to play King Richard," she muttered to Olivia.

"Too round," the older woman pronounced, shaking her head.

"Okay, people, let's get to work!" Adam called, and immediately the set was buzzing with activity.

Adam seated himself in the director's chair as the crew began staging one of the four battle scenes. On film, the action would last for four minutes, but the work that went into the scene lasted all day. They rehearsed portions of the scene over and over again. At the same time, the assistant director was staging a bit of action that would later be cut into the main action. Everywhere Bridgette looked something was going on.

Finally Adam was ready to go through the entire sequence. Bridgette watched as he skillfully directed the extras, some on horses and others on foot, toward their places. At last what looked like two opposing armies faced each other across a wide stretch of desert sand. Adam shouted instructions through a megaphone, and the armies began to advance slowly.

At that moment he called for the camels, which had been kept downwind of the horses since, Bridgette knew, camels couldn't abide the smell of horses. She and Adam had discussed his plan to carefully monitor the direction of the wind and the movement of the animals. By keeping the horses downwind and out of sight until the last minute, he hoped to use both sets of animals in the same scene.

Bridgette held her breath and prayed that Adam's plan would work. For a while she thought he'd made it. The opposing armies continued to advance, the horses' bridles glinting in the hot sun, the camels and their Arab riders looking regal and exotic.

Then, suddenly, the wind picked up, and all hell broke loose. Bridgette stared stupefied as the terrified camels took off in all directions, their riders transformed at once from kingly Arabs to shocked actors who clung to their mounts. In an instant the horses were following suit, their shrill screeches rending the air as they pawed the ground nervously, then bolted every which way, sending crew members running for shelter. People screamed in fright as they narrowly missed the horses' pounding hooves.

Bridgette and Olivia fled a safe distance away and watched from Bridgette's trailer steps. She scanned the scene, looking anxiously for Adam, and her heart lurched painfully when she spotted him in the midst of the pandemonium, shouting instructions through the mega-phone. She watched terrified as a riderless horse galloped by.

Then she recognized Sindee by his side. Adam yelled something to her and pushed her away. She began run-ning awkwardly, her legs getting tangled in her costume, then she tripped and fell headlong into a large water trough, missing a camel by mere inches. The same camel careened right into the lunch wagon, upsetting a carefully arranged display of food and trampling mounds of fruit and vegetables.

"At least we'll be spared a ghastly lunch," Olivia remarked dryly.

Bridgette didn't comment. She stared dumbfounded as props, chairs, and equipment were all scattered or smashed beneath the hooves of the stampeding animals.

Great clouds of dust filled the air and impeded her vision, but above the din she began to hear Adam shout-ing orders to the animal trainers and their assistants. "Get those animals separated!" he yelled. She watched as most of the horses fled the camp and disappeared behind a hill. Adam groaned. "Not that separated!" He directed the head trainer to a car and jumped behind the wheel of a jeep, spinning the wheels in the sand as he gave chase to the lead horse.

Bridgette sighed with relief as the scene quieted and people began emerging from their hiding places. Sindee rose from the water trough looking like a drowned kitten, her hair hanging in matted clumps down her back, and her costume clinging to her, torn and dirty.

Just then Bridgette caught sight of Beamish standing safely off to one side, taking copious notes, probably for his nightly call back to Davidson, Bridgette surmised.

"I'd like to make him eat that notebook," she told Olivia.

"And send him home with indigestion," the older woman agreed.

Hours passed before Adam returned in the jeep, a string of docile horses in his wake. He was covered with dust from head to foot and looked very tired. Bridgette's heart went out to him. Forgetting to hide her real feelings, she ran out to meet him as he got out of the jeep. "Are you all right?" she asked anxiously.

Adam's eyes brightened when he saw her, and he nodded wearily, giving her a sheepish smile. "Well, I learned something today. No more trying to integrate the horses and the camels—at least not *these* horses and camels," he added with a laugh.

He always could find the humor in a situation, Bridgette thought fondly.

Adam glanced at his watch, then jumped up on the jeep's running board. A small crowd had already gathered around him. He grinned and called out, "Cut!"

A wave of laughter rose from the group, and Bridgette sensed the tension being lifted.

"Ralph, are there any injuries to report?"

"Just minor cuts and bruises—and one ruined costume," he answered looking meaningfully at Sindee, who had changed into the first practical clothes Bridgette had seen her in since they'd arrived. "There was some damage to equipment, but we should be able to manage with what we have for the next day or two, until we've had a chance to replace the broken parts."

"Good," Adam answered. "I think we're all pretty

lucky. That's all for today, people. We'll make a fresh start tomorrow."

"But there are still several hours of daylight left, Reeves," Beamish insisted, pushing people out of his way as he approached the jeep. When Bridgette refused to give him ground, he glared at her and walked around her.

"By the time we set up, it'll be dark," Adam said firmly, climbing down and walking past Beamish, who fell into place beside him.

"The assistant director stopped working the minute you left the set," Beamish reported. "Totally unprofessional."

Bridgette could see that Adam was struggling to keep his temper. "The assistant director had nothing to direct, Mr. Beamish," he said. "The horses were all going south while the camels were all going into each other. We are not filming a disaster picture—although," he added under his breath, "it might turn out that way yet." Leaving Beamish mutely opening and closing his mouth, Adam called "Ralph!" and Ralph appeared. "Come with me to my trailer. I'll describe tomorrow's shooting schedule while I shower. Bridgette!"

"Yes, B'wana," she said, arriving at his side. He put a grimy arm around her slim shoulders and for a moment it was almost like old times.

"The script changes?" Adam asked.

"Part done," she answered with a smart salute.

He laughed and rubbed his neck in a weary gesture. "Bring them around in forty-five minutes—and bring your hands," he added as she began walking away.

"What?"

"I need a massage."

Seeing the twinkle in his eye, she suppressed her amusement and said, "It's not in my job description."

"Ralph will have it in the contract by the time you come back," Adam promised, mounting the steps to his trailer and disappearing inside.

Bridgette turned, smiling happily, and walked right into Pamela.

The woman's hair was arranged in a beguiling up-sweep, and she wore a pretty sundress that exposed a lot of bare skin. Bridgette's hand rose to one of her pigtails, and she said nothing. Pamela looked Bridgette over from top to bottom, and there was a certain sadness in her eyes. Then she turned and knocked on Adam's trailer door.

Without looking back, Bridgette walked deliberately to her own trailer some forty feet away. In the background she heard Pamela say huskily, "It's me, Adam."

An hour and a half later Bridgette finally walked over to Adam's trailer. She was wearing a pair of the jeans he had bought for her and a very brief tube top that hugged her body. Her hair lay in short tousled wisps about her face. She knocked on the door forcefully, then entered without waiting for a reply.

Adam was sitting on a small sofa in front of a twenty-six-inch television set that he used to view the daily rushes. It was the most imposing piece of furniture, other than the bed that peered out of the back room.

"You're late," he told her, rising.

"Are you alone?" she asked icily.

"Yes. See, no hidden girls in the sugar bowl." He lifted the lid for her inspection.

"I wasn't sure if your girlfriend had left yet," Bridgette said, her voice brittle.

"Ralph?" Adam asked with a laugh.

"Pamela," she said firmly.

"Pamela brought my story board back to me," he said, indicating the huge notebook on his desk. "I'm making some changes."

"So what else is new?" she asked. "Well, here are your new pages," she said, dropping them onto the table and turning to leave.

"What's your hurry?" he asked, his voice low and husky.

She'd never been able to resist that voice. It enfolded her, filling her with warmth, calling to the part of her that leaped in response to his touch.

"I've got some more work to do," she said.

"Got a man lined up?"

His comment caught her off guard, and she was honest before she could think not to be. "You know better than that. I mean—"

"Then stay awhile," he urged, reaching up and running his hand ever so lightly against her thigh. The heat of his hand seared right through the material and seemed to scorch her leg. Ripples of excitement began to run through her almost immediately, and she felt her legs grow weak, unable to support her.

"I—"

"Will stay," he said. "Say it. I will stay. Not very hard for an English major," he teased.

"Well..."

"Don't you want to see the rushes?"

She was experiencing her own rushes at the moment, and they had nothing to do with the film.

He pointed to the television set and the videocassette recorder on top of it. "I thought you might like to see how some of your new dialogue looks on film."

"All right," she agreed hesitantly. His hand was resting on her hip, sending dangerous signals through her body.

"Sit down," he coaxed.

"What?" she asked, dazed.

"You know, bend your knees and let your body drop down in a chair."

"I know what sit down means," she snapped.

"Good, then do it. Right here." He patted the place next to him on the sofa.

She looked around, but there really was no other place to sit other than at the table, which was awkward for viewing the set. Adam smiled as she took her seat, trying to sit as far off to the side as possible. He slid in closer to her. From the cabinet next to him on the right he pulled out a bag of popcorn.

"Remember the old days when we were dating?" His grin was engaging, and she couldn't help smiling.

Adam turned on the set with his remote control and then ran the rushes. For a few minutes they sat quietly watching Joel and Sindee. To Bridgette's surprise, Sindee was actually delivering her lines with feeling and conviction. Bridgette was impressed and decided that Adam could get a good performance out of a corpse.

Gradually she realized that while she was watching the rushes, Adam was watching her.

"I thought we were going to view the rushes," she said, increasingly conscious that there was now no space between them on the sofa. Adam had showered and was wearing a light-blue shirt with the sleeves rolled up and the buttons undone half-way down. Bridgette yearned to touch the hard muscles of his chest.

"I've already seen the rushes," he told her.

"You've already seen me, too," she answered dryly. "Why are you watching me?"

"Because you're much more exciting than anything I've ever seen on film." He took the bag of popcorn from her hands and drew her into his arms.

"Adam, please don't," she said, looking away just as he was about to kiss her.

He let go of her slowly. "Have it your way," he said pleasantly. "I never forced you."

Force me, force me, a little voice cried inside of Bridgette. But she rose to go.

"Hey, I said I needed a massage," Adam reminded her, stopping her with one glance.

"I thought Pamela took care of that for you," Bridgette said coolly.

"Nobody can do it like you," he said, and his words carried a thousand and one meanings to her.

"Okay," she said, resigned. "Turn around."

"Uh-uh," Adam said, shaking his head, a mischievous smile on his lips. "We have to do it right." He led her into the bedroom, turning on one dim lamp.

Bridgette regarded him warily. "This is just going to be a massage," she clarified, on her guard.

"Of course." Adam stripped off his shirt.

She stared at his rippling muscles. How was it that he held her captive every time he moved?

Adam lay face down on the bed, and she stared at his broad back. He was teasing her, playing a game of cat and mouse. Well, she'd show him. She began kneading his back with a vengeance, her fingers strong and un-wielding.

"Hey, hey, you're not kneading bread. I'm an expensive director. Be gentle."

"Gentle doesn't do the trick," Bridgette said as she strove to massage him even harder.

Adam half turned toward her, but she pushed his head back down into the pillow, twisting his neck expertly. She had gotten to be quite a good masseuse.

Adam groaned. "A little bit of strong-arming, then?" he asked archly.

"That'll do the trick," she said, thinking he meant the massage.

Suddenly he flipped over onto his back and pulled Bridgette down on top of him. "You're the boss," he said wickedly.

"Adam, what are you doing?" she demanded, trying to push away from him but finding that she could sooner fly than get out of his viselike grip.

"Following orders," he said innocently.

"Are you crazy?" she cried, still struggling.

"Maybe just a little." He seemed to consider the question, then conceded, "Maybe a lot." He kissed the hollow of her throat.

"Adam, please..." Bridgette pleaded, her voice growing softer as she struggled less and less. The feel of his hard body beneath her sent a flame of arousal through her.

"You don't have to beg me," he teased, his kisses fanning out, forming a Y that pointed directly down to her cleavage.

"Why you big, conceited oaf, you—" Words failed her.

"You're going to have to rewrite that dialogue," he

told her, wiggling her body so that her tube top came free and her breasts pressed against his smooth, hard chest. His hands were on either side of her, rubbing her breasts, igniting a fire within them. Then one hand slipped between them, the light hair on his arm tickling her as her flesh tingled and sizzled.

With one motion he turned her onto her back and was looming over her, his eyes flashing promises of heaven as they caressed her all over.

"Is this the way you always view the daily rushes?" she asked with difficulty.

"Not with Ralph," he told her, his head lowering once again, his lips savoring her breasts.

"But with Pam—"

Adam's head snapped up. "Shut up, Bridge. You talk much too much." He covered her mouth with his own.

He kissed her, over and over again, his hands stroking her tenderly, drawing out the inner flames that burst forth in tongues of fire all through her. He covered all of her in a light veil of smoldering kisses. Even her eyelids felt hot as his lips brushed gently past them.

Bridgette listened to his heavy breathing, and her own breathing quickened in response. He wanted her, her heart sang, anticipation pulsating so hard through her body that she thought she would explode. His fingers slipped down her jeans and tugged at the heavy snap, then pulled down the zipper. He pulled at the material, but it refused to budge.

His kisses lessened and then his grinning face hovered over her. "Have you been training your jeans?" he asked. "They're fighting me."

"Something has to."

"Why?" he asked, rising on one elbow and then rocking back on his heels, kneeling in front of her and pulling at the stubborn jeans.

Bridgette made a feeble attempt to stop him, but her heart wasn't in it, and Adam calmly pushed her hands away and drew the jeans down to her thighs, then leaned down to kiss the inside of each thigh before sliding away the remaining material.

"There," he said in a voice that throbbed with desire, "that should take care of resistance." He tossed the jeans in a heap on the floor. His eyes held Bridgette fast as he stretched out his long, powerful body against her, half covering her with it and half holding back.

Slowly, languidly, he ran his hand over her smooth, firm body, which tensed against his touch yet arched toward it. Bridgette thought she would grow mad with wanting him. What was he doing with her? She could hardly stand waiting . . . waiting . . .

She reached up and, entwining her hands into his thick hair, pulled his head down to her, kissing him forcefully, passionately, while within her head flares of fiery lights sailed off into the far corners of her mind's eye.

His hands slipped inside her panties, and he slid them down over her hips in an impatient motion.

"You're still dressed," she protested, the words a dry whisper in her throat.

"Here," Adam said, guiding her hand to his belt buckle. "Now you do me."

"Ever the director," she murmured huskily against his mouth, but she followed his instructions eagerly. She managed to free the belt buckle with one hand, then deftly unhooked his trousers. And then, with no effort at all, the material slid away, leaving nothing but small briefs between them, which quickly disappeared by her own hand.

Her boldness surprised her and seemed to intensify Adam's excitement. As his breath grew lower and deeper she felt his desire grow.

"Oh, Bridgette, Bridgette," he said in a voice that was hoarse with passion. He raked her hair with his hands, and pulled her mouth to his as his body covered hers completely, bringing ecstasy back in such force that Bridgette could barely breathe.

Their entwined bodies rocked to an inner music that passion created within them, pushing heaven and earth away as they climbed higher and higher into paradise. The spiral that pulled Bridgette ever upward snatched her last breath away as a moan tore from her throat. She heard her own voice cry out Adam's name. She thought she heard herself say, "I love you." Or did he say it?

She had ceased to think; she could only feel. Sensations cascaded throughout her. Nothing registered except the racing of her pulse and the hot trail of his lips and hands over her body. She was poised on the brink of ecstasy.

A hot knife tore through her, followed by brilliant colors shooting wildly about. And then, slowly, clinging to him, Bridgette floated back to earth. Adam held her protectively and kissed her, but softly now.

"You look beautiful when you smile."

"Am I smiling?" she asked in a small voice.

"Like a happy child." He pushed the hair out of her eyes and drew her to him once again.

10

IN THE FOLLOWING week Bridgette felt as if she was half in heaven, half in hell. She was painfully confused about everything. When she was in Adam's arms, everything was perfect. But out of them, she was once more plagued by doubts, jealousies, and the thought that Adam didn't really need her. She wanted desperately for him to need her . . . to love her.

But Adam was preoccupied with trying to bring the picture in on time, and had little time for her. The animals had cost them some time, and then the weather had turned inclement. They lost hours waiting for high winds to die down so that they could resume filming.

One day Bridgette watched as they set up a scene in which the principle actors were supposed to gather about a campfire at night. The cameras were all set with filters, and the exposure levels were turned down to facilitate the filming. Suddenly dark clouds began to gather, threatening a rain storm.

Sindee, lying in the arms of the leading actor, looked up at Adam in the middle of her love scene and cried, "Cut!"

Adam came up to her, his patience clearly growing thin. "Sindee," he said as she rose from her reclining position, aided by Adam's hand. "I'm supposed to say that. It's my right as the director. It's getting to be my only pleasure," he added wearily.

"Well, I don't have any pleasure," she pouted. "Not with this dialogue. Adam, honey, I can't say these words!" she complained dramatically.

Bridgette felt her temper flare. "Why?" she snapped at Sindee. "Aren't there enough monosyllables in it for you?" It was all she could do to put up with Adam's criticism. Sindee's was more than she could stand.

Sindee's eyebrows knitted together in a scowl. "She wrote these silly words on purpose!" she cried to Adam. "Where's the magnetism? Where's the sexy, provocative words?"

"I thought that was your part," Bridgette cut in sweetly. "Aren't you an expert at conveying sexiness?"

"Not with words that sound like I'm ordering a ham sandwich!" Sindee spat out, coming at Bridgette with her fists clenched.

Adam quickly intervened. "Settle down," he ordered. "Bridgette," he said, his tone firm, "Sindee has a point."

Bridgette stared at him in consternation. She had admitted privately that the scene was not her strongest, but to be criticized by someone she disliked, and then to have Adam join in against her, was too much. "Just what do you mean, *she's right?*" Bridgette demanded.

"I haven't felt comfortable about the scene either. His dialogue is fine"—Adam gestured toward the leading actor—"but Sindee's is rather—"

Don't let him say that word, Bridgette thought.

"Stilted."

Sindee seized immediately on the word. "I can't act with stilted dialogue!" she said, waving her hands.

"You can't act, period," Olivia threw in from the sidelines. Bridgette flashed her a grateful smile.

But Adam wasn't ready to yield. Just then there was a rumble of thunder and a smattering of raindrops. Adam sighed and looked heavenwards. "Well, that clinches it. *He* doesn't like the scene either." He glanced back at Bridgette, who was struggling to hold back another angry retort.

She'd been right all along, Bridgette thought. Adam had taken this job just to humiliate her. How better to do that than by siding with Sindee?

"You," Adam was saying, pointing to Sindee, "go to your trailer. I don't want you getting wet and catching cold. I can't afford to let that hold up production. And you—" he said, turning toward Bridgette.

"—go rewrite the scene," she supplied, mimicking his voice. "It doesn't matter if *I* catch a cold."

"Yes it does," Adam said softly once Sindee had left. "I'll rub salve on your chest to make you better," he promised with a twinkle in his eyes. "Or at least make *me* better. Now be a good girl and do your thing."

"I already did my thing," she retorted.

"Well, do it again. Give her something believable to say."

"I don't know if I can write that simply."

"Try," Adam called after her.

Bridgette slammed the door of her trailer.

Adam came to her trailer that evening bearing a peace offering—a complete roast beef dinner that he'd had Ralph bring in from the city. But Bridgette would have none of it. "I'm not hungry," she said coldly, hardly looking at him.

"Now what are you angry about?" Adam demanded, his own temper rising.

"You sided with her," Bridgette accused him, hurt sounding in her voice despite her intent to sound aloof. She rose to face him.

"Mind if I put these plates down?" he asked. "My hands are beginning to char." He placed the platters on the table, then turned to her. "There are no sides, Bridge," he insisted.

"Oh, aren't there?" she asked sarcastically. "Then why did you agree with Sindee?"

"Because for once in her life she was right."

"What does she know about good dialogue?" Bridgette demanded indignantly.

Adam shrugged. "She got lucky. Now for goodness sake, stop taking it all so personally!"

"I can't help it. I *personally* wrote those lines!"

Adam closed his eyes, as if drawing on an inner strength. "Damn you, Bridgette, sometimes you make me crazy—and sometimes," he said in a voice that dropped two octaves and was soft and tender, "you make me crazy."

"Oh no, not this time, Romeo," she said, backing away. "This time you're not using that lethal mouth of yours to make me do what you want. I'm not jumping through hoops like some trained seal."

"That's not quite what I had in mind," Adam said with a sexy smile. But he made no move toward her. Only his eyes pulled at her, eyes that could trap and hold her and make her do things against her conscious will.

"I know what you plan to do," she accused him. "You plan to kiss me until I'm a puddle, have your nightly exercise, and then leave me at my typewriter, doing your bidding."

"One thing has nothing to do with the other," Adam said, sounding less amused. "I want you to rewrite Sindee's dialogue for the good of the picture."

"Oh, *the good of the picture* again," she said wearily, a slight edge to her voice. Her eyes strayed to the plates he had set down. She had to admit that she was hungry.

"Look, if Sindee comes out looking like a fool—" Adam began.

"It would be right in character," Bridgette interjected.

"Granted." He grinned. "But then the whole picture will suffer," he pointed out. "Besides," he added, this time coming up behind Bridgette and enveloping her in his arms, "that dialogue is yours. I don't want anyone making fun of your efforts."

Was he serious? She wanted to believe him, but she had trusted him once before, and it had resulted in nothing but pain.

"Now sit down and eat with me before everything gets cold and dried out," he ordered.

"I'll eat with you," she said, taking a seat opposite him but still watching him carefully, "but I won't play with you."

"We'll see." He began to eat, then said conversationally, "It wasn't supposed to rain today. Not even supposed to rain much this month. Sometimes I think the gods are against me. Well," he said, his eyes dancing merrily, "at least they brought you back into my life."

His words warmed her heart, but she could tell from his light tone that he wasn't really serious. He was just saying what he thought she wanted to hear. It annoyed her that he was sure of her reaction to him. It almost gave her enough incentive to keep away from him. Almost, but not quite.

Ralph came to her rescue. "It's one of the cameras," he told Adam, rushing into the trailer.

"Well, at least it's not one of the camels again," Adam said, rising to follow him.

"It's worse. A wet camel smells bad, but it can still operate."

"Who the hell left the camera out?" Adam thundered as he left the trailer.

Bridgette sighed. Another order of business had taken him away from her just as he had made her want to yield to him. She was saved . . . or was she?

Yes, she told herself, rising suddenly and clearing away the dishes, she was saved. She didn't want to be his plaything. She wanted to be his helpmate, not just a flunky following orders. Orders. She glanced over at the typewriter. Well, she was getting paid to do the job, so she might as well get on with it.

Sitting down at the typewriter in earnest for the first time that day, Bridgette began to rewrite the scene. No one else had ever made her do so many changes before. The script didn't even look like the original *Desert Serenade*. All those changes were slowing them down, as would the damaged camera, no doubt. Who had left it out? she wondered. Had someone done it on purpose?

She sucked in her breath as the thought suddenly came to her. She crossed over to the small window and looked out, catching sight of Adam disappearing around a corner. Heavy raindrops splashed onto the windowsill. Not wanting to continue her line of thinking, Bridgette let the curtain fall into place and went back to work.

They got a new camera from the studio, the delay setting them back a day, and resumed filming at a faster pace in order to make up the lost time. Adam was everywhere—overseeing rehearsals, making sure that the assistant director got his work done, and redoing several scenes on the story board as Bridgette handed him the changes he'd requested. Still, despite additional setbacks—an actor fell off his horse and cracked a rib and one of the other supporting players sustained a deep cut during the rehearsal of a duel—filming stayed on schedule.

Their success did not keep Beamish from popping up at every opportunity to offer bad advice, making everyone edgy. It seemed to Bridgette that whenever she looked over her shoulder there he was watching her. The others seemed to feel the same way.

"I can't take it anymore, Adam," Rex told him at the end of the second week, just when they were about to shoot the climactic battle scene. "Either that weasel goes, or I do!"

"He's too round to be called a weasel," Adam said.

"Look, Rex"—he put his arm around the smaller man's shoulders—"please just hang in there a little while longer. I need you."

I need you. How Bridgette longed to hear him say those words to her, she thought as she stood with Olivia, filling a lull in the afternoon by watching the activity on the set.

Rex shrugged. "Okay, okay, but keep him away from me."

"I'll talk to him, Rex, I promise. Right now, just think of him as your cross to bear, okay?"

"I'm Jewish, Adam," Rex said as a parting shot.

Bridgette tried not to laugh.

Later that day Bridgette finished several more pages and, feeling good about how things were going, decided to deliver the pages to Adam in person. She walked briskly over to his trailer, despite the afternoon heat, and was about to knock when she heard voices through his open window. She recalled hearing Ralph mention earlier that Adam's air conditioning had broken down. At the time, it made her smile wryly. Now she felt perfectly serious. The voice she heard was Pamela's.

Ever so quietly Bridgette walked away from the door, toward the window. She didn't care if anyone saw her listening.

"Adam, I know you're under a lot of pressure right now," Pamela was saying in her sweet, unhurried voice— a voice so different from her own, Bridgette thought. "I just want you to know that I understand if you're a little gruff toward me." Gruff? He had been the personification of patience, Bridgette thought, biting her lip. "I still love you, and I know you love me." The words ripped at

Bridgette's heart. She didn't even realize for a moment that tears were welling up in her eyes.

"Pamela—"

At the sound of Adam's husky voice, Bridgette couldn't bare to stay. She hurried back to her own trailer, relieved to see Olivia was still gone, and sat down numbly on the bed, staring into space.

For the next few days filming went on as before, with the cast and crew trying valiantly to bear up under further strain and discomfort. One of the stunt men was injured when his horse rolled on top of him. Then the weather turned nasty again. Finally the sun came out once again, and Bridgette thought they were in the clear.

They began filming action scenes several miles from the main camp. Bridgette had come, along with Olivia, curious to see how her scene worked visually. They were in the third jeep, with Bridgette driving. She was finding it difficult to control the vehicle in the loose sand.

"Be careful," Olivia chided when Bridgette made a sharp turn and narrowly missed overturning the jeep.

Bridgette focused ahead once again—and was horrified to see the wheels of the first of the open trucks plunge down a steep embankment. The vehicle flipped over, tossing the camera and crew into the air like rag dolls before landing in front of several oncoming horses and riders. Pandemonium broke loose as the riders strained to keep their terrified horses in check. One animal narrowly missed clipping a cameraman on the head with his flying hooves.

Adam, who was closest to the action, ran toward the truck and, to Bridgette's horror, dashed in to pull out the driver as flames began to shoot from the vehicle.

As Adam pulled the driver back from the fire, Bridgette rushed over to him, arriving before the rest of the crew.

"Are you all right?" she cried, kneeling with him next to the unconscious body.

Adam nodded, his concerned gaze on the driver. Ralph came just then with a car to take the injured man to the hospital. As several of the crew members fought to put out the fire, Adam and Ralph lifted the driver into the back of the station wagon.

"You want to come along and have that looked at?" Ralph asked, nodding toward Adam's arm as he slipped into the driver's seat. Shocked, Bridgette saw that Adam had been burned and scratched.

Adam shook his head. "It's all right," he said, and Ralph gunned the motor and sped away.

"All right, my foot!" Bridgette objected, stepping in. "Hal, get me the first-aid kit," she called over her shoulder to one of the grips, who stood nearby. "Someone else get me a chair." She examined Adam's arm and shook her head. The blond hair was singed. Her heart was still pounding from thinking what could have happened to him.

Two folding chairs appeared as if out of nowhere. Members of the crew crowded around, anxious to know if Adam was all right.

Bridgette opened the battered first-aid kit someone had thrust into her hands.

"There's no alcohol," she cried. "Olivia!"

The older woman pushed a path through the crowd. She regarded Adam with concern. "You okay?" she asked him.

"Of course he isn't okay," Bridgette retorted before

he could speak. "Get me your flask of whiskey out of the jeep."

Olivia nodded and made her way back through the crowd.

"Olivia still nips, eh?" Adam said with a grin, then added, "Bridgette, I wish you'd quit fussing over me."

"I'll be out of your way soon enough," she said, her voice cool. "Right now you can stop being Mr. Terrific for a minute. As soon as I finish, you can walk across a bed of nails and prove to everyone how manly you still are." Just then Olivia returned with a canteen.

"What a waste of good whiskey," Adam muttered as Bridgette poured some on his arm. He winced.

"It's rotgut," she said, beginning to wind bandages around his arm.

"It's medicinal," Olivia protested, standing next to her.

"You know," Bridgette said to Adam, unmindful of the people crowding about them, "you could have been fried to a crisp." She glanced over at the charred and twisted heap of metal that had been a truck only minutes before.

Just then Beamish arrived at their side. "Reeves, does this mean the picture is going to fall behind schedule?" he demanded, mopping his sweaty brow and scowling.

"No, Mr. Beamish," Adam said, and Bridgette saw smoldering anger in his eyes. "The picture will not fall behind schedule. Despite all that God and nature have contrived, the picture will stay on schedule. We may even have five minutes to spare," Adam assured him coldly, "provided Florence Nightingale here doesn't tie me into a knot." His expression softened as his eyes met Bridgette's.

"Don't tempt me," she said, finishing off the bandage and glaring at Beamish. Suddenly she felt Adam's free hand on her wrist, the pressure chiding her from saying anything. She looked back at him and for his sake held her tongue, although she was itching to give Beamish a piece of her mind.

"Adam, are you all right?" Pamela asked breathlessly, emerging from the ring of people just as Bridgette had sat back to close the first-aid kit.

Bridgette glanced up to see a look of deep concern in the other woman's eyes. Then, remembering what she had overheard earlier in Adam's trailer, she slipped quietly away. The crowd closed around Adam as people began firing questions at him.

Olivia grabbed Bridgette's elbow. "Hey, what's the matter with you?" she demanded as Bridgette put the first-aid box into the back of their jeep.

"Hmm?" she asked, pushing the hair out of her eyes.

Olivia gave her a stern look. "You just walked away like a dog with its tail between its legs. What gives?"

Bridgette shrugged. "I did my part. I bandaged his wound. Pamela can take care of the rest."

Olivia stood staring at Bridgette as the sun beat down on them. "And that's it?" Olivia demanded. "You're throwing in the towel—again?"

Bridgette sighed and leaned against the jeep, deliberating facing away from Adam and the crowd. "There is no *towel*, Olivia," she said. "There's nothing left between Adam and me."

"If you think that, you're dumber than I thought," the housekeeper retorted, shaking her head. "You keep that up and I'll have someone else adopt me," she threatened.

"No one else would put up with you," Bridgette replied, smiling fondly in spite of herself. "Well," she added with a sigh, "time to get back to work."

This time the pang in Bridgette's heart wouldn't go away.

11

DESPITE THE NEAR tragedy, filming resumed as usual with Adam at the helm. Bridgette was relieved to hear from Ralph that the driver Adam had saved was well on the way to making a full recovery.

She spent the next few days watching Adam work, vowing to herself that this was the last time they'd work together. In her heart she was sure that Adam and Pamela would eventually get married, and she wanted to spare herself the pain of being around when it happened. She was absorbing as much of Adam as she could while keeping a safe distance. He hadn't asked her for any more changes in the script and, for once, filming was going along smoothly.

Adam was a master, she thought. He always managed

to get the best work out of his people, whether they were
no-talent, hollow beauties like Sindee or unsure new-
comers like Joel.

Joel had blossomed before their eyes. He performed
his small part remarkably well. He definitely stood out,
Bridgette thought, and she knew he'd go far.

With things going so well, Bridgette relaxed her guard
quite a bit. She was therefore unprepared when Adam
approached her the following Tuesday just after lunch.
"Want to go scouting for a location with me?" he asked.

Startled, she looked up from her lapboard, where she'd
been trying to piece together thoughts for another screenplay. She was sitting under the canopied canteen, although lunch had been cleared away. Shading her eyes,
she studied Adam for a moment. His golden head was
framed against the blue sky, and her heart filled with
longing at the magnificent sight of him.

"You want to go in this heat?" she asked.

"If I wait for the heat to dissipate, we'll be filming
in November. Or in the middle of the night." He crouched
down next to her chair. "Aaron is taking care of this
afternoon's shooting. I need a site where Saladin and
Richard can confront one another. Why don't you come
along?" He grinned engagingly at her.

In this position her eyes were level with his, and she
felt she was drowning in them. "What about Rex?" she
asked. "I thought he was supposed to help you with this
sort of thing."

"Rex is in his trailer. I gave him a little time off. His
nerves are frayed."

She nodded almost absently, acutely aware of all the
reasons why she shouldn't go, but already giving in to

her desire to be alone with him just once more. Adam was running his hand up and down her thigh. "Beamish on Ralph's case again?" she struggled to ask.

Adam nodded, then rose, holding out his hand. "Come with me?" he asked softly.

The invitation sounded so seductive. Bridgette was sure Adam could read the phone book out loud and make it sound like a proposition.

She fought to bring *no* to her lips, but no sound came.

"The way I see it, you're the best suited to tell me if the location coincides with what you had in mind when you wrote the scene."

"What I had in mind when I wrote the screenplay never seemed to matter to you before," Bridgette said, thinking of all the pages he had crossed out since they'd arrived. But she rose anyway, careful not to take his offered hand.

Nonetheless, he placed his hand against the small of her back and guided her toward the open jeep. She looked at it in dismay.

"Can't we take the air-conditioned car?" she protested.

"I need four-wheel drive."

"I need the studio back lot," she said miserably, climbing in and putting on her sunglasses.

"You wrote the script," Adam reminded her.

"Next time I think I'll write about Mickey Rooney staging a benefit to save the local high school," she muttered.

"That's Andy Hardy," he corrected, dropping a canteen of water into the back seat, on top of a worn blanket that had been left behind.

"Whoever." She sighed. "No more far-off locations

for me—unless it's Hawaii. But with my luck," she added as they sped away, "the volcanoes would probably all erupt while I was there."

"That's what I love about you"—Adam laughed as they drove toward the Lakeside Mountain area—"you're such an optimist."

_"Some things," Bridgette said glumly, thinking of Adam and Pamela, "you just know are fated."

Adam let the subject drop. "Lord, it's good to get away from Beamish," he said.

"Are you sure you're really away from him?" Bridgette said, glancing around. "He might be hiding under the blanket, taking notes."

"I already checked," Adam assured her, a note of seriousness in his voice. "Just you and me, kid."

"And the iguanas and the scorpions and the black widows and the—"

"You have a way of ruining the best scenarios," he told her, laughing.

"Not me," she protested as they plowed over the hot sand, toward shimmering mountains that rose up in the distance like majestic guardians of the sky. Already the camp was just a dot behind them. They were surrounded by miles and miles of sand under the merciless sun.

"Now what are you implying?" Adam asked. "Are we going back to the broken record you keep playing?"

"It's not a broken record," she again protested. "Are you going to marry her?" she asked suddenly, not able to contain herself any longer.

"Which _her_ are you referring to?"

"How many women are you planning to marry?" she asked, attempting to sound light.

"None. But you think I'm mixed up with so many women, I was just curious to know which one had finally managed to win me."

"You know very well whom I mean. Pamela," she said tensely, watching her face.

"Boy, have you got the wrong number," he said, laughing.

"You're not going to camouflage it by making light of the situation. I heard you."

Adam stopped the jeep and stared at her. "Heard what?" he demanded, his voice deadly serious.

"Look, I don't want to talk about it," Bridgette said, looking away.

Adam turned her forcefully to face him. "That's what went wrong the first time. You stopped 'wanting to talk about it,'" he told her. "I never knew what was wrong until it exploded in my face in little gurgled phrases!"

"I don't gurgle!" she protested indignantly.

"You don't make any sense either."

She shrugged, trying to maintain what little dignity she had left. "I'm sorry if I'm not like Pamela."

"Pamela again," he said in exasperation. "Are we going to talk in code all afternoon?"

"We don't have to talk at all!"

"Oh, yes we do, lady. Now what does Pamela have to do with it?" he demanded.

"Everything," Bridgette said, trying to hold back sudden tears. Why was he playing games with her like this? What was to be gained? Wasn't he satisfied that she still cared for him, that she came to him when he beckoned? How much more did he want from her?

Without thinking clearly, Bridgette jumped out of the

jeep. But Adam followed and grabbed her roughly. "If you're thinking of walking back, don't," he warned sternly.

"Give me a little credit," she retorted.

"I'll give you more than a little if you'll talk to me. Now what's all this about Pamela?" he demanded, grasping her shoulders as if to squeeze the truth out of her. "What did you hear?"

Bridgette raised her chin high. "I heard Pamela tell you that she loves you."

"What?"

Bridgette sighed, all at once tired. "The other day I was walking by your trailer and your window was opened. I heard Pamela tell you that she loves you and that she knows you feel the same about her."

"Oh," Adam said, as if everything had fallen into place.

"Yes, 'oh,'" Bridgette echoed. "So, if you have any of that Iowa niceness left in you, you'll leave me alone."

But Adam wasn't about to be put off. "If you heard that, why didn't you stay for the rest of it?"

"Because I didn't want to hear you tell her you love her," she admitted, then stopped. "How did you know I walked away then?"

"Because, my sweet, if you had stayed you would have heard me tell Pamela that I was very flattered, very touched, and very sorry, but I was still in love with my ex-wife."

"If you expect me to believe that—" Bridgette began, then stopped, stunned into silence.

"Yes, I do expect you to believe it, Bridgette." His brilliant green eyes caressed her as he pulled her into his arms. He kissed her. He pressed her against the side of the jeep. She felt the heat of his loins as he molded himself to her body. Tears slid down her cheeks as she savored the sweet flavor of his lips.

Adam loosened his hold and looked down at her for a long, long moment. She could see that he was struggling to keep himself in check. Finally, he sighed deeply. "Let's get on with this before I forget why I'm here," he said, a husky lilt in his voice.

He helped her back into the jeep, and she dried her tears, somehow feeling better than she had in a long time.

They drove for a while in silence, until they approached a place that Adam pronounced as perfect. And it was, Bridgette had to agree. A cavern provided a perfect background for Saladin's warriors camp, and an open area in front would be a good place for the two leaders to meet.

Adam turned to her. "Okay?"

"Okay," she confirmed, then smiled. "It's nice to have my opinion matter."

"Everything about you matters," he assured her, taking her hand. "Let's explore."

"I'd rather just look at it at a distance," she said, shaking her head.

"We're not going to get lost. I'm a former boy scout."

"Nevertheless, I'm not wandering around there without a bunch of pebbles to drop on the ground so we can find our way back," she said firmly, refusing to budge.

Adam sighed and got back behind the wheel. "Sometimes I wonder why I bother," he said. "You just refuse to enjoy the beauties of nature."

"Not so!" she objected. "I just like to see them from a distance, all neat and clean and without any creepy crawlies." Sincerely afraid of getting lost, she waited for him to start the jeep.

Which he didn't. Or rather couldn't.

A whining noise assaulted Bridgette's ears as the engine refused to turn over. She looked at Adam in alarm. "Now what?"

"I don't know," he said, trying the key again.

"Don't tell me we're out of gas. I won't believe that." There was a hint of panic in her voice.

"It's not the gas," he said, getting out and flipping open the hood.

Bridgette joined him reluctantly and stood looking down at the mysterious metal parts that meant nothing to her. From the look on Adam's face, they apparently meant nothing to him, either.

"Well?" she asked.

"It won't go," he said.

"That sounds very technical."

"Look, what do you want? I was the only guy in my town who didn't come alive taking apart old engines. If my brother were here, he could fix it with his eyes shut."

"If Donna were here, she'd probably just lay her hands on it and heal it," Bridgette muttered in frustration, more to herself than to him. Then, realizing what she'd said, she glanced at Adam to see his reaction.

"How is Donna?" he asked casually, still staring at the engine.

"She went to Europe on the arm of a duke. She's probably worked her way up to king by now." Bridgette paused. "How come you didn't keep up a correspondence with her?"

Adam looked surprised. "Why should I?"

"Well, you got along so well when she was out here,"

Bridgette said, her voice becoming slightly heated with the painful memory.

He shrugged. "She was part of your family. I made an effort."

"It looked to me like you were making more than that."

Adam regarded her carefully. "I'll be honest with you," he said. "Your sister came on to me rather intensely. I'd never met two women who were as different as you and your sister."

"Yes," Bridgette said, looking off into the distance. "She's got it all."

"What *all?*" he asked. "Beauty? That only goes skin deep, remember?"

"Most people consider it enough." She sniffed.

"I don't," he said quietly. "I like brains and spunk." His eyes twinkled. "As long as the spunk gives in to me." Then a thought seemed to hit him. "Bridgette," he said slowly, "did you think I was interested in your sister?"

"Weren't you?" she asked hesitantly. "She seemed to think so." Her voice dropped as she added, "She told me you were."

"And you believed her?" he asked incredulously.

Bridgette shifted her attention to a lonely Joshua tree that stood before them, its sharp, bayonetlike leaves hanging from large, clumsy branches. Then she looked down at her feet.

"You believed a person who, by your own admission, went out of her way to make you feel inferior?" Adam insisted.

"Then why were you so nice to her?" she demanded.

"Because I thought I might help heal the rift between you. I hadn't counted on how shallow Donna was—or how insecure you turned out to be."

Bridgette shrugged, feeling the fight suddenly go out of her. "That goes back to the womb. Donna didn't kick. I did," she said with a small smile.

"And you're still kicking." He laughed.

For a brief moment she laughed, too. Then she grew serious once again. "Yes, I guess I still am." She took a deep breath, as if to push back all memories. "Okay, now that true confessions are over with, what do we do?"

"It'll be dusk soon. I guess we'll have to wait for help, or until this thing decides to rise up from the dead," he said, kicking a tire.

She glanced at the sky. "When do the vultures come?"

"Not for at least half an hour," he told her, keeping a straight face. "Don't worry, Beamish won't let me stay away from the set for long. He's got everything down to a science."

"Yes, like how long you're supposed to take for a nervous breakdown. Yesterday that man tried to tell me how to write," she told Adam, shaking her head in disbelief.

He grinned broadly. "I bet he was sorry."

Remembering, she felt pleased with herself. "I think he was at that." Her expression grew sober. "And now instead of putting Beamish in his place, I'm here with you."

"Here alone, together," Adam said, putting an arm around her shoulders.

"With little critters," she corrected, looking down at a black bug that was burrowing back into the sand. How many more little black bugs were buried there she wondered, her skin crawling.

"Why don't you concentrate on the big critter instead?" Adam suggested, turning her to him.

"The iguana?" she asked, teasing.

"Bigger," he prodded. "C'mon, now you have no excuse. We can look at the cave." And with that, he pulled her along.

"How soon do you think they'll come looking for us?" she asked, running to keep up with him.

"Very soon."

"Very soon, huh?" Bridgette said, echoing his words an hour later as the sun sank slowly toward the horizon. They were standing exactly where Adam intended King Richard and Saladin to meet, but Bridgette felt like less than royalty as she gazed out at miles of beige sand that was turning dark beneath the dimming curtain of night. Above them shone a pale moon.

"Even the stars have gone out," she muttered. "They probably moved to a better neighborhood."

"Come here," Adam coaxed, patting the place next to him on the blanket, which he'd spread out at the mouth of the cave. As she settled down next to him, he offered her the canteen, which was getting very low. She pressed it to her dry lips, savoring the wetness, then handed it back to him.

"I guess we'll have to spend the night here, huh?" she said miserably. She had never camped out before. She didn't like being outdoors. Right now even the trailer sounded good to her.

"Looks that way. Don't worry. They'll be here by daybreak."

"What happened to 'soon'?" she asked, not liking the

darkness that was gathering so quickly around them.

"It's been replaced." He grinned. "A rewrite," he added, his voice low as his fingers trailed slowly across her cheek. "I'm kind of glad they won't be here soon."

"This does appeal to you, doesn't it?" she said, glancing around the cave.

"Not half as much as you do."

He offered her half a stale sandwich that he had discovered in the back of the jeep. She accepted it, munching slowly, surprised to find she wasn't hungry. The desert was slowly going to sleep around them. It was so still, as if there was no one else left in the world except for the two of them, and an eternity of sand. Bridgette felt strangely peaceful. She leaned her head against Adam's shoulder as she swallowed the last morsel of food. His arms went around her shoulders and he turned her head toward him. The peacefulness she felt was suddenly replaced by a fire of love and longing. A quiver of anticipation went through her as he kissed her, deeply, longingly. At last he raised his head and gazed down at her.

"What if someone comes?" she said with effort.

"We'll hear them first," he promised, stroking her hair, his breath sending a warm shiver through her. "Cold?" he asked.

"I'm finally not hot anymore," she said. For some reason she was having trouble speaking.

He kissed her temples lightly. "You're not hot?" he echoed mischievously, his eyes shining in the fading twilight.

"You know what I mean," she said, embarrassed at her verbal clumsiness.

"Then I must be doing something wrong." He pulled her closer still.

"No, the formula's working," she admitted reluctantly as she felt his hands gliding along her arms.

"Goose bumps," he said in surprise. "Mine or the desert's?"

She heard the grin in his voice. "What do you think?"

He lifted her chin with one finger. "I think that as director it's my duty to look out for your welfare."

"Then why did you bring me out here in a dying jeep?"

"To drag you off to my secret lair and have my way with you." He leered. "Since the castoff blanket we have does little to warm our chilling bones, I'll make the supreme sacrifice of covering your body with my own."

"How?" she asked, waves of intense excitement beginning to ebb and flow within her.

"How do you think?" he asked, pushing her back onto the blanket and stretching out next to her.

There was no chill in the night air. Somehow, after a moment, even the desert faded away as Adam's hands began to weave their magic. To her surprise, as her clothing fell from her body, she became warmer. She no longer worried about being found by someone. All she cared about was having Adam make love to her, having him want her just once more. Tomorrow seemed light-years away, and ecstasy lay just beyond her fingertips, beckoning to her in waves of ever increasing warmth.

Adam explored her body slowly, thoroughly as if discovering her for the first time. His kisses had long since set her ablaze with yearning, but still he took his time, deliberately prolonging the pleasure they were sharing.

Bridgette unbuttoned his shirt and murmured something to him. She felt his throaty laugh rumble in his chest, which pressed ever so sweetly against her breasts, his smooth skin rubbing maddeningly against her hard nipples. She tugged at his shirt sleeve, and he looked quizzically down into her face.

"You, too," she said, her voice a whisper choked with desire.

"Obligingly." He shrugged out of his shirt.

"Pants," she commanded.

"Most willingly." He laughed, squirming out of them, moving enticingly against her. The strong contours of his body further aroused her growing appetite. His hands moved toward his brief shorts, but she reached to stop him. "I'll do it," she said. He raised himself on his palms, over her, his face almost on top of hers, and his mouth brushed against her face as she slipped the last shred of clothing down his thighs.

"You finish," she said, hardly able to stand the pulsating sensations that danced demandingly through her.

"Gladly," he said, and the word held many promises for her.

Their lovemaking was unlike anything she had ever known before. Adam took her with urgent, demanding heat. He took her once, then again, and yet again, making heaven and paradise explode for her in a crescendo of overwhelming passion.

As she came slowly back to herself, descending from dizzying heights while still savoring feelings of lingering magic, Bridgette turned her face to Adam. He pulled the blanket over them, making a cocoon. She reached out to touch his face.

"You're smiling," she said.

"I always smile when I'm happy. It's one of my strange quirks."

"Are you happy?" she asked languidly, fatigue creeping over her.

"If I were any happier"—his voice caressed her in the darkness—"they'd put me away."

"Adam?"

"Hmm?"

"What if they don't find us?"

"They'll find us."

"But what if they don't?" she persisted.

"Then they'll find us like this, with smiles on our faces."

She turned slightly to peer out at the black sky. "I wish the stars would come out," she said in a small voice.

His hands tightened about her waist, then slipped down her thigh in slow, arousing movements.

"I can make them come out again," he told her softly. And he gathered her close to him once more.

12

"THEY'RE COMING!" BRIDGETTE cried, bolting upright.

It was dawn and already hot. From her vantage point at the cave's entrance she could see great clouds of dust formed by moving jeeps. Within minutes the vehicles stopped and she heard far-off voices calling to them.

Adam opened a sleepy eye, his blond hair falling into his face. "Damn," he said. "No time for one more taste of heaven." He grinned at her wickedly.

At once she realized that he wasn't looking at the advancing procession, but at her breasts, which were fully exposed to his vision, the blanket having fallen away when she sat up.

"Oh, you!" she cried, jumping up and snatching up her clothes.

"That's not the way you sounded last night." He chuckled, rising also and swiftly putting on his discarded jeans and shirt.

He turned back to look at her as she leaned against the wall of the cave, pulling on her jeans. Suddenly his face turned white, and before she could ask him what was wrong, he leaped inside the cave and pulled her aside. She stumbled and fell, bringing him down with her. He groaned and grabbed his arm.

"Adam, what is it?" Bridgette cried. He turned to face her, holding his arm awkwardly. "Did you break it?" she asked, searching for a sign.

And then she saw it. Scurrying under a rock as picturesquely as if it were part of an insect science film was a black widow spider. She immediately recognized its distinctive shape and red markings. She must have disturbed it when she'd accidentally kicked over a rock.

Bridgette sucked in her breath. "Oh, Adam," she cried again, her cool fingers touching the red welt that was already forming on his arm, just above the bandage.

He bit his lip. "Not too lucky lately, am I? Maybe you've got something there about not being too crazy about nature," he said, trying to joke. But she could see that he was in pain.

"Help will be here in a minute, darling," she said, and she ran out of the cave in her bare feet. The men had already reached their jeep when she cried out to them. They looked up in surprise and immediately came running.

Within an hour they were back in camp. Adam was already running a high fever, and Bridgette insisted that they take him to a doctor. Both Adam and Beamish opposed her request.

"We only have five days of shooting left," Beamish insisted. "We can't stop now. As the studio's representative, I insist that—"

"Stuff it," Bridgette interrupted angrily as they stood in Adam's trailer. "He's going to a hospital."

Adam waved a hand at Bridgette from where he lay on the bed. "Just get the doctor to come out here," he said. "I know what I'm doing."

"I doubt that," she said, her angry tone masking her fear. "Oh, all right," she relented. "But I'm not going to stand here and argue while you get sick and die. Ralph!"

"I'm on my way," he said, already out the door.

Olivia joined Bridgette a few minutes later. She stared down at Adam, looking thoroughly distressed. "Is it bad?" she asked, not taking her eyes off Adam's face, which was flushed and damp with perspiration.

"It's not good." She bit her lip.

Olivia grew pale. "I'm sorry, Adam," she said.

Adam closed his eyes and nodded imperceptibly, barely moving his head.

Bridgette looked at her. "What do you mean, you're sorry? You didn't put the spider there. If anything, it's my fault. He pushed me out of the way."

"No, it's my fault," Olivia insisted miserably. "I told him to do it."

Bridgette was thoroughly confused. "Told him to do what?"

"To take you out into the desert and pretend to get lost. Ralph was supposed to 'find' you this morning. I thought if you spent a night alone together, you'd be able to patch up your differences." Her voice trailed off as she looked down at Adam, who seemed to be slipping into unconsciousness.

At another time Bridgette might have chastised Olivia for interfering in her life, but she knew her friend felt horribly guilty. Besides, things *had* turned out wonderfully for them. They had cleared the air about so many things. But what if Adam didn't make it?

Bridgette slipped her arm around Olivia's slight shoulders. "He'll be all right," she promised, trying to convince herself as well.

"Worst reaction I've seen in a long time," the doctor told Bridgette sometime later, after he had examined Adam. "Although I've heard of a few people dying," he added, doing nothing to raise her spirits. Bridgette hoped the man knew what he was doing. Ralph hadn't been able to find anyone else willing to come.

"We should take him back to Salt Lake City and get him into a hospital," the doctor continued.

"No, no hospital," Adam said, waving his hand weakly.

The balding man shook his head. "First, I'm practically kidnapped by this man," he said, gesturing to Ralph—"I promised him a king's ransom," Ralph told Bridgette, who nodded knowingly—"and then my advice is overruled. Well"—the doctor sighed—"I'll send someone out with the necessary medicine." He turned to Bridgette. "Keep him warm and in bed until the fever passes. And make sure he drinks plenty of liquids. Drown him if you have to. He'll be all right," he added, casting a wary eye over Adam's long frame.

Bridgette nodded, and even Adam managed a small smile. "We can do what we did last night," he said, already drowsy from the injection the doctor had given him.

"Later," Bridgette said, turning her attention to the departing doctor. "Thank you for coming," she said.

The gruff man nodded. "I didn't have much choice," he said. His expression softened as he stepped outside the trailer and looked around at the milling actors and actresses. "Are you really making a movie here?"

"We're trying," Bridgette said. "God knows we're trying."

She went back inside to find that Adam had fallen asleep. A shiver went through her. What if he did die? What if he was taken from her just when things had fallen into place for them at last?

"Later," she said out loud. "Right now, we've got a picture to worry about."

She was afraid that without Adam Beamish would try to take over the set, which would undoubtedly cause havoc. But Adam couldn't possibly direct. An idea began to form. She pushed back the hair from Adam's forehead. "Maybe just this once," she whispered, "you're going to need me again."

In half an hour she was back outside viewing the turmoil that was beginning to ensue. Without Adam to guide them, the crew members were at loose ends. Usually in such cases the assistant director would step in to quell the problems until the director returned or the studio sent in a replacement. But, although Aaron was a talented director, Bridgette had learned from watching him in the preceding weeks that he wasn't a commanding leader. He was still very unsure of himself and now seemed grateful when Beamish began telling him what to do.

Ralph looked at Bridgette helplessly. "We're in for it now," he said as she stepped down the trailer steps.

She watched Beamish gesture vaguely around him. He was loudly vetoing the location Adam had staked out yesterday for the confrontation between the two leaders in the movie. The scene could take place right where they stood, near the lunch wagon, Beamish said. Or even on the studio back lot.

"With fake sand," Bridgette suggested sarcastically, coming up behind him.

He turned and regarded her disdainfully.

Rex, who had been arguing with Beamish, began to stomp away. "I'm quitting, Ralph. I've had it!" he shouted, throwing up his hands and walking off the set in a huff.

"Let him go. There's no room for a prima donna!" Beamish said with a grand wave.

"He's the best in the business, Mr. Beamish," Bridgette said firmly. "Ralph, please talk to him when he cools off." The production manager nodded.

Beamish looked peeved at Bridgette's assumption of authority. "*I'm* here now," he said. "We don't need Rex and his ego."

"He's worked on several award-winning movies," she said. "What have you worked on?"

He pursed his fleshy lips. "*Space Invaders* and *Venetian Spring*," he told her haughtily. "They were released last year."

"Those weren't released, Mr. Beamish, they escaped." A titter of amusement rose from the small group of camera operators who were waiting for instructions.

"Young woman, I will not stand here and be criticized by a hack writer! Don't forget that your career is on the line, too. Now, I have an important job to do." He was about to push past her and issue another order, but Bridgette put a restraining hand on his shoulder.

"Your job, as I understand it," she said evenly, "is to watch, and observe, and to step in if something drastic happens to hold up production."

"Well, something drastic has happened!" he insisted. "Reeves—"

"—has given me a series of orders to be carried out," she interrupted, adding cheerfully, "He may be flat on his back, but there's nothing wrong with his mind."

His thick eyebrows rising, Beamish looked toward Adam's trailer. "I'll just see about that," he said, about to go off.

Bridgette put out her hand to stop him. "I left him sleeping, Mr. Beamish. The more rest he gets, the faster he'll recover."

"But I should be the one who's told—" Beamish sputtered.

"All in good time, Mr. Beamish, all in good time," she soothed. "Now, we don't want anything to get in the way of our keeping on schedule, do we?" she asked sweetly, then turned toward Aaron. "Adam wants you to take the crew and do Scene 138. You'll use the locale he scouted out yesterday. Ralph can show you where it is."

"Me?" Aaron asked in disbelief.

"You're the assistant, aren't you?" she asked, smiling at him encouragingly. "Adam says it's time for you to try your wings."

A smile began to spread over Aaron's face. "I guess it is at that," he said. "Okay, men, you heard the boss. Let's roll."

Bridgette stood back, pleased with herself. Beamish was still muttering and shaking his head, but he apparently didn't doubt that Bridgette was acting on Adam's authority.

But Ralph looked at her curiously, his expression amused. Bridgette winked at him, then hurried to her trailer to get her notes on the rest of the script.

She spent the rest of the day and part of the evening in Adam's trailer, poring over his story board, which Ralph had left behind for her. Adam didn't give her much trouble—he slept comfortably for most of the afternoon.

Working quickly, Bridgette went over the various notes in the margins of his script and applied them to the changes that he had intended for the story board. Unlike some directors, Adam changed the story board constantly, taking and discarding many ideas in the course of filming. Only after a scene was shot did he consider the drawing final.

"Here," Bridgette said that evening, thrusting the story board into Ralph's hands. "These are the scenes to be filmed tomorrow."

"Adam's orders?" Ralph asked, hiding a smile.

"Absolutely," she said solemnly. "How did it go today?"

"I think Aaron's drunk with triumph—also beer," Ralph said, jerking a thumb toward the canopied area where the recently returned crew was eating a late supper.

Bridgette heard their rousing chant. "Half a liter, half a liter, half a liter onward," Aaron sang, as he lifted his glass of beer.

Bridgette laughed. "Well, at least they're happy."

Just then Beamish walked by, shaking his head.

"Drunken sots," he muttered, climbing the steps to Adam's trailer.

Bridgette all but jumped into him to keep him from entering. "Sorry, Mr. Beamish, but he's resting again and can't be disturbed." The fat man gave her a sour look and waddled off without saying a word. "Film's on schedule, Mr. Beamish," she called gaily after him. Then she sighed, glancing at Ralph. "Two more days before Adam should be fully recovered."

"You can do it," Ralph said, giving her an encouraging pat on the back.

Somehow she did manage. She organized the shooting schedule, kept Beamish at bay, and took care of Adam all at the same time. By the morning of the third day things were going more smoothly than she had dared to hope.

"But I should be out there," Adam protested, putting down his breakfast tray and beginning to rise.

Bridgette put a restraining hand on his chest and found that she had to use two hands. He was getting stronger. "It's going well," she assured him. "Ralph, Aaron, and Rex are handling everything. One more day won't hurt."

"But Beamish—"

"—is being kept in his place. Trust me."

Adam still looked uncertain. "What about the shooting schedule?" he asked.

"The film is doing fine, really. You've trained everyone so well that they're carrying on just swell without you. You know, doing one for the master."

"I've got a strange idea I know who the 'master' is." Adam's eyes mocked her.

"Just rest," she told him. "At this rate we'll be able to pack up tomorrow and go back to civilization. Here, take your medicine." She rose to get the bottle from his nightstand.

Adam laughed and opened his mouth, then made a face as he swallowed a spoonful. "Did you sleep here last night?" he asked, taking hold of her hand.

"And the night before that," she said, pulling free and putting the cap back on the bottle.

"Too bad I couldn't take advantage of the situation." He grinned.

"There's a first time for everything," she returned glibly. "Besides, I was just guarding you from your many fans. Everyone's tried to come in here at least once. Promise you won't go over the wall? Or do I have to leave Olivia guarding you? She's dying to cook you something."

Adam sank back down against the pillows. "I'll be good," he promised with mock docility.

"Now you're learning," Bridgette praised him, kissing him swiftly on the lips, then stepping outside.

She got busy with the day's work. The assistant director needed very little prodding, and the day's filming was completed sooner than she'd expected.

Bridgette sighed with relief. Tomorrow Adam would be strong enough to take control again and she wouldn't have to run interference between Beamish and everyone else.

A small tug of sadness pulled at her heart. Tomorrow Adam wouldn't need her anymore. She pushed the thought away as she headed for her own trailer.

Bridgette was surprised to find Joel waiting for her. He was still dressed in his costume and looked quite different from the young waiter they had met just a few weeks ago. Today he looked far from shy. In fact, he carried himself with such an air of debonair confidence that Bridgette began to wonder if he was going "Hollywood."

"Hi," he said in a sleek voice.

"Hi, yourself," Bridgette answered, entering her trailer. Joel followed.

"I've been waiting for you," he said to her lazily as he closed the door behind them.

"Have you now?" she asked. "And why is that?" She circled around to the other side of the table, thinking it prudent to keep something between them. She didn't like the look in his eyes.

"I thought we could talk—about my career," he answered in a husky voice.

"Okay," she agreed. "Let's talk. You first."

"Adam has you making a lot of changes in the script, doesn't he?"

So, it was "Adam" now, was it? "Yes, what about it?"

"Can you write a bigger scene for me?" Joel asked, his eyes never leaving her face.

"I suppose I could, but he . . ."

Joel came closer to her. "Something that would let me show off my full potential," he told her, his eyes gleaming. He came even closer, as if he was stalking her. "I'd be terribly grateful." His face just inches away from hers, he ran the tips of his fingers along her cheek.

"I've no doubt," she said dryly, "but Adam hasn't asked me to rewrite your scenes." She stepped back.

But Joel wouldn't be put off. "He's your ex-husband, isn't he?" he insisted, following her.

"What of it?" she replied testily, growing more and more annoyed.

"You could, um, *make* him consider the matter, couldn't you?" Joel suggested meaningfully.

Bridgette had had enough. She pushed him away from her. "Just who do you think you are, buster?" she demanded. "I'm not going to be hustled into furthering your career or anyone else's! I'll excuse you this time. Maybe your head's in a tailspin over this whole picture, but nobody buys me or tries to use me. And I'm not in the market for grateful favors. Do I make myself clear?"

To her surprise, Joel kissed her hard on the mouth.

At the same moment, the trailer door opened, and Adam came in.

Joel sprang back guiltily. Bridgette stared at Adam, wide-eyed. "What are you doing up?" she demanded, shaken.

"Apparently seeing things I wasn't supposed to see. Sorry for intruding," Adam said sarcastically, and he turned on his heel and walked out, slamming the door behind him.

Bridgette shot a murderous look at Joel as a feeling of helplessness overwhelmed her. "Now look what you've done!" she cried. Without giving Joel a second glance she ran after Adam.

He was disappearing into his trailer by the time she reached the bottom step of hers. Joel, she noted with relief, did not follow her. Damn him, anyway! What a time for Adam to walk in. Why hadn't he come in two minutes earlier, when she'd been telling Joel off?

"Adam," she called, knocking, but there was no response. Determined to confront him, she threw open the door and walked in. She found him stripping off his clothes, the shower water already running for a shower.

"Your tryst over so soon?" he asked mildly. "Must have been rather disappointing."

"What tryst?" she demanded. "Joel was trying to seduce me, hoping to get me to write him a bigger part."

"Uh-huh," Adam said, obviously not believing a word she said.

"It's true," she insisted, taking hold of his arm. "Adam, it wasn't what it looked like."

"You don't owe me any explanations, Bridgette. What you do with your time is your own business. If you want to make love to every pretty face that comes your way—"

"I wasn't making love! I was—" Abruptly, she stopped. His words had an all too familiar a ring to them. A thought suddenly flashed across her mind. "Why you, you—"

Adam grinned at her. "What?"

"You set me up!" she cried.

"Me? Would I do a thing like that?" he asked, placing a hand on his chest in mock outrage.

"Damn straight you would!" she shot back.

"How does it feel to be accused when you're totally innocent?" he asked, smiling triumphantly. He chucked her under the chin.

She was about to deliver him a scathing set-to, but something made her change her mind. "It feels awful," she admitted, seeing the humor in the situation for the first time. "Okay, I deserved that."

"You bet you did—tenfold," Adam said, pulling out a yellow plush towel from the bottom of a crammed drawer. He glanced up at her, but she turned away, unable to meet his penetrating gaze. "Let's make a deal, okay?"

"What?" she asked, still wary.

"For now—and for always—I want you to promise me that before you let your fertile little brain make assumptions about any given situation, you talk to me first, okay? And I'll try to cherish what I have," he told her, raising her chin with a gentle finger and looking deep into her eyes. "Ralph told me what you've done for me," he said. "I'm really surprised you pulled it off, and deeply touched. But on the other hand, I always knew there was something special about you."

She shrugged, feigning an unconcern she was far from feeling. "I couldn't let your picture fall into Beamish's hands. He could undo in three days everything you'd done in three weeks. Besides, it was nice having you need me for a change—even if you were unconscious half the time."

Adam kissed her lips briefly, then went into the bathroom. "I've always needed you," he said softly.

"What?" she said, stepping closer. "The water's running. I can't hear you."

"I said I've always needed you. I never stopped needing you."

"Sure, sure. What could I do for you once you'd become successful? You already had a secretary. You already had a manager. You didn't need me to tell you how good you were. Everyone else was doing that."

He came out of the bathroom with a short towel neatly tucked against his tanned, taut abdomen. "I don't need you to sew on my buttons or run my set incognito, although it was nice of you to do that for me. I *do* need you for my soulmate."

When she said nothing, he put his hands on her shoulders and looked her straight in the eye. "Remember all those old grade-B westerns where the old gunslinger says to the new gunslinger that there'll always be someone who's faster than him?" She nodded, not understanding what he was driving at. "Well, there will always be someone who's prettier than you—"

She flinched, but he held her fast.

"—or more intelligent than you. And maybe there's even someone out there who's more short-tempered than you are. But there'll never be anyone who's you. And you're the only one I want. Then and now. Forever. Do I make myself clear?"

She nodded slowly. "Does that mean you really do love me?" she asked in a trembling voice, needing to hear the words.

"That means I'm willing to spend the rest of my life trying to make you get over your damned insecurities. And this time I won't let Hollywood go to my head," he promised. He picked up something from the bureau and held out a tissue-wrapped item in his hand. "I saved this for you."

She opened it gingerly. Tears filled her eyes as she recognized the wedding ring she had flung at him when she discovered him with Rhonda.

"It took me three days of combing my trailer to find it," he said. "I always hoped I'd have a chance to give it back to you. I even arranged to be made director of the film and then asked for extra rewrites so you'd have to spend more time with me."

"Sometimes I suspected as much," Bridgette admitted. "But I thought you wanted to get even with me for leaving you. I thought I'd wounded your ego."

He laughed and began unbuttoning her blouse with sure, swift fingers. "I didn't want to get even, Bridge," he said huskily. "I just wanted you back."

Bridgette blinked back her tears. "All this trouble for me?" she said in disbelief.

"I thought you were worth it," Adam replied, taking off her blouse and unzipping her jeans.

She stepped out of them in a daze. "Then why didn't you just tell me?"

"You and your damned defenses. You never let me. But I'm telling you now," he said, unhooking her bra.

"Adam, what are you doing?" she asked, suddenly realizing that she was standing before him almost totally naked, that he had been undressing her as they'd talked.

Adam scooped her up in his arms and carried her into the bathroom. "I'm getting ready to give you a bridal shower," he said brightly. "You never had one the first time." He deposited her on the floor outside the stall and pulled off his towel. "Coming?" he asked, stepping inside.

"You too?" she asked uncertainly.

"Why not? I never had a bridal shower either."

She laughed and stepped quickly out of her panties and into the shower. "It's cramped in here," she said.

The grin on Adam's face grew wider as water beaded on his muscular frame. "The word is *cozy*, Ms. Screenwriter."

"Yes, it is, isn't it?" she murmured.

His eyes held hers once again. "I love you, Bridgette."

"Oh, Adam, I love you so much."

And his arms enfolded her in a warm and lasting embrace as she closed the shower door behind them.

_____ 06401-7 **PRIMITIVE SPLENDOR #41** Katherine Swinford

_____ 06424-6 **GARDEN OF SILVERY DELIGHTS #42** Sharon Francis

_____ 06521-8 **STRANGE POSSESSION #43** Johanna Phillips

_____ 06326-6 **CRESCENDO #44** Melinda Harris

_____ 05818-1 **INTRIGUING LADY #45** Daphne Woodward

_____ 06547-1 **RUNAWAY LOVE #46** Jasmine Craig

_____ 06423-8 **BITTERSWEET REVENGE #47** Kelly Adams

_____ 06541-2 **STARBURST #48** Tess Ewing

_____ 06540-4 **FROM THE TORRID PAST #49** Ann Cristy

_____ 06544-7 **RECKLESS LONGING #50** Daisy Logan

_____ 05851-3 **LOVE'S MASQUERADE #51** Lillian Marsh

_____ 06148-4 **THE STEELE HEART #52** Jocelyn Day

_____ 06422-X **UNTAMED DESIRE #53** Beth Brookes

_____ 06651-6 **VENUS RISING #54** Michelle Roland

_____ 06595-1 **SWEET VICTORY #55** Jena Hunt

_____ 06575-7 **TOO NEAR THE SUN #56** Aimee Duvall

_____ 05625-1 **MOURNING BRIDE #57** Lucia Curzon

_____ 06411-4 **THE GOLDEN TOUCH #58** Robin James

_____ 06596-X **EMBRACED BY DESTINY #59** Simone Hadary

_____ 06660-5 **TORN ASUNDER #60** Ann Cristy

_____ 06573-0 **MIRAGE #61** Margie Michaels

_____ 06650-8 **ON WINGS OF MAGIC #62** Susanna Collins

_____ 05816-5 **DOUBLE DECEPTION #63** Amanda Troy

_____ 06675-3 **APOLLO'S DREAM #64** Claire Evans

_____ 06680-X **THE ROGUE'S LADY #69** Anne Devon

_____ 06687-7 **FORSAKING ALL OTHERS #76** LaVyrle Spencer

_____ 06689-3 **SWEETER THAN WINE #78** Jena Hunt

_____ 06690-7 **SAVAGE EDEN #79** Diane Crawford

_____ 06691-5 **STORMY REUNION #80** Jasmine Craig

All of the above titles are $1.75 per copy

Available at your local bookstore or return this form to:

SECOND CHANCE AT LOVE
Book Mailing Service, P.O. Box 690, Rockville Cntr., NY 11570

Please send me the titles checked above. I enclose _____ .
Include 75¢ for postage and handling if one book is ordered; 50¢ per book for
two to five. If six or more are ordered, postage is free. California, Illinois, New
York and Tennessee residents please add sales tax.

NAME _____

ADDRESS _____

CITY_____ STATE/ZIP_____

SK-41

Allow six weeks for delivery.

_____ 06692-3 **THE WAYWARD WIDOW #81** Anne Mayfield

_____ 06693-1 **TARNISHED RAINBOW #82** Jocelyn Day

_____ 06694-X **STARLIT SEDUCTION #83** Anne Reed

_____ 06695-8 **LOVER IN BLUE #84** Aimée Duvall

_____ 06696-6 **THE FAMILIAR TOUCH #85** Lynn Lawrence

_____ 06697-4 **TWILIGHT EMBRACE #86** Jennifer Rose

_____ 06698-2 **QUEEN OF HEARTS #87** Lucia Curzon

_____ 06850-0 **PASSION'S SONG #88** Johanna Phillips

_____ 06851-9 **A MAN'S PERSUASION #89** Katherine Granger

_____ 06852-7 **FORBIDDEN RAPTURE #90** Kate Nevins

_____ 06853-5 **THIS WILD HEART #91** Margarett McKean

_____ 06854-3 **SPLENDID SAVAGE #92** Zandra Colt

_____ 06855-1 **THE EARL'S FANCY #93** Charlotte Hines

_____ 06858-6 **BREATHLESS DAWN #94** Susanna Collins

_____ 06859-4 **SWEET SURRENDER #95** Diana Mars

_____ 06860-8 **GUARDED MOMENTS #96** Lynn Fairfax

_____ 06861-6 **ECSTASY RECLAIMED #97** Brandy LaRue

_____ 06862-4 **THE WIND'S EMBRACE #98** Melinda Harris

_____ 06863-2 **THE FORGOTTEN BRIDE #99** Lillian Marsh

_____ 06864-0 **A PROMISE TO CHERISH #100** LaVyrle Spencer

_____ 06865-9 **GENTLE AWAKENING #101** Marianne Cole

_____ 06866-7 **BELOVED STRANGER #102** Michelle Roland

_____ 06867-5 **ENTHRALLED #103** Ann Cristy

_____ 06868-3 **TRIAL BY FIRE #104** Faye Morgan

_____ 06869-1 **DEFIANT MISTRESS #105** Anne Devon

_____ 06870-5 **RELENTLESS DESIRE #106** Sandra Brown

_____ 06871-3 **SCENES FROM THE HEART #107** Marie Charles

_____ 06872-1 **SPRING FEVER #108** Simone Hadary

_____ 06873-X **IN THE ARMS OF A STRANGER #109** Deborah Joyce

_____ 06874-8 **TAKEN BY STORM #110** Kay Robbins

_____ 06899-3 **THE ARDENT PROTECTOR #111** Amanda Kent

All of the above titles are $1.75 per copy

Available at your local bookstore or return this form to:

SECOND CHANCE AT LOVE
Book Mailing Service, P.O. Box 690, Rockville Cntr., NY 11570

Please send me the titles checked above. I enclose _____.
Include 75¢ for postage and handling if one book is ordered; 50¢ per book for
two to five. If six or more are ordered, postage is free. California, Illinois, New
York and Tennessee residents please add sales tax.

NAME _____

ADDRESS _____

CITY_____ STATE/ZIP_____

Allow six weeks for delivery.   **SK-41**

WHAT READERS SAY ABOUT
SECOND CHANCE AT LOVE BOOKS

"Your books are the greatest!"
— *M. N., Carteret, New Jersey**

"I have been reading romance novels for quite some time, but the SECOND CHANCE AT LOVE books are the most enjoyable."
— *P. R., Vicksburg, Mississippi**

"I enjoy SECOND CHANCE [AT LOVE] more than any books that I have read and I do read a lot."
— *J. R., Gretna, Louisiana**

"I really think your books are exceptional . . . I read Harlequin and Silhouette and although I still like them, I'll buy your books over theirs. SECOND CHANCE [AT LOVE] is more interesting and holds your attention and imagination with a better story line . . ."
— *J. W., Flagstaff, Arizona**

"I've read many romances, but yours take the 'cake'!"
— *D. H., Bloomsburg, Pennsylvania**

"Have waited ten years for *good* romance books. Now I have them."
— *M. P., Jacksonville, Florida**

*Names and addresses available upon request